CW00405239

CHRISTMAS CHAOS

KELLY KAY
EVIE ALEXANDER

EMLIN
PRESS

First Published in Great Britain 2022 by Emlin Press in conjunction with Decorated Cast, LLC.

Copyright © Kelly Kay & Evie Alexander 2022

The moral right of Kelly Kay & Evie Alexander to be identified as the authors of this work has been asserted in accordance with the Copyright, Designs and Patents Act of 1988.

All rights reserved. No part of this publication may be reproduced, stored in a retrieval system, or transmitted in any form or by any means, electronic, mechanical, photocopying, recording, or otherwise, without the prior permission of both the copyright owners and the above publisher of this book, except for the use of brief quotations in a book review.

All characters and events in this publication, other than those clearly in the public domain, are fictitious and any resemblance to real persons, living or dead, is purely coincidental. All brand names and product names used in this book are trademarks, registered trademarks, or trade names of their respective holders. Emlin Press is not associated with any product or vendor in this book.

ISBN (eBook) 978-1-914473-12-8

ISBN (Print) 978-1-914473-13-5

A CIP catalogue record for this book is available from the British Library.

www.emlinpress.com

EMLIN
PRESS

To Charlie and Elway and the hope that they'll always believe.

NOTE TO READERS AND
CONTENT WARNING

A heartfelt holiday greeting from Evie and Kelly.

Happy, Merry Everything!

Welcome back to EVIE & KELLY'S HOLIDAY DISASTERS, full of madness, mirth, and steam. They're hilarious side-by-side novellas with interconnected characters, focusing on one holiday and one trope at a time.

6 Stories

6 Happily Ever Afters

3 Holidays

3 Tropes

2 Time Zones

2 Authors

Multiple disasters

And 1 Asshole Monkey

<u>Volume One Holidays & Tropes</u>

Valentine's Day - Insta-Love
Fourth of July - Friends to Lovers
Christmas - A visit with old friends from our respective writing
universes

CHRISTMAS CHAOS, the third and final book in Volume One can be read as a standalone, but is more fun if you've read Cupid Calamity and Cookout Carnage first. Both are available on Amazon and free in Kindle Unlimited.

With Christmas Chaos, we essentially go home for the holidays with our beloved characters from our individual universes. Rory, from Evie's Kinloch series, and Tabi, from Kelly's 5 Families Vineyard Series, get their shot at a different type of happily ever after, each with their own partners, of course. And the rest of the Airport Lounge six will be involved in the disasters as much as they can.

Giving birth to this series was a labor of love (total pun- read on, and it will be super funny once you've read this book). It was much more fun than we thought it would be. It was also harder than we thought it would be, not just working with each other across time zones but creating a believable and engaging world where this madness made sense to the reader. But at the end of the day, we're insanely proud and excited by this series and thank you for embracing it with such open arms.

Christmas Chaos is the marriage of Evie (a Brit), with Kelly (an American). Evie writes in UK English and Kelly in US English. So if you see colour instead of color, realising instead of realizing, and " around dialogue rather than "", please know it is meant to be written that way!

CONTENT WARNINGS!

Here's something we didn't anticipate when writing Holiday Disasters - content warnings!

Seriously though, both of our stories revolve around pregnancy and some difficulties around it. There are fertility issues, a suspected miscarriage, and hospital visits. We both write happily ever afters, but for anyone who's ever experienced miscarriages, difficult pregnancies, or fertility issues, we wanted to make sure you were aware we deal with these subjects.

These situations are personal to us, and even though these novellas are works of madcap farce, they're grounded in some of our realities. But as always, we try and see the bright and humorous side of things.

Wishing you the best of the season and Happy Holiday Disasters to all of you,
xo
Evie & Kelly

Ps - If you want access to book information, graphics and elements for you to use on your social channels, please help yourself to our Media pack: https://eviealexanderauthor.com/ christmas-chaos/

❧ I ❧
NO WAY IN A MANGER

By
Evie Alexander

PROLOGUE

February 12 – Chicago, IL
United Lounge, O'Hare Airport
2:27 p.m. CST

R ory MacGinley, the Earl of Kinloch, was as far out of
his comfort zone as the Loch Ness Monster in an
aquarium.

He was surrounded by strangers in a lounge at Chicago
airport. Not only did they want to engage him in conversation,
they were also drunk. Rory hadn't touched alcohol in years.

His entire trip to the States had been a lesson in accep-
tance and biting his tongue. Having promised his mother he
would visit her and her new husband, he'd left his beloved wife
and the peace and quiet of the Scottish Highlands to travel to
a country where everyone talked far too loudly and way too
much.

Tabi Aganos, one of his brand new acquaintances, was a

case in point. She appeared to have taken the most raucous parts of her Greek heritage and mixed them with the most exuberant parts of her American one. The result was a woman who could waltz into a graveyard, wake the dead, and have them conga out onto the streets within minutes. She was currently wearing an empty wine box around her hips and strutting as if on a catwalk.

'Yo, Bagpipes! Does this make me look fat?'

Rory ignored her.

The wine had come from Tabi's Sonoma vineyard, Prohibition Winery, and considering the rate it was being consumed it must have been delicious. Sabrina, a small blonde American, was the furthest gone, with Brits Tristan and Ben following closely behind. The least inebriated were Tabi, who seemed to have an inbuilt tolerance, and Jonathan, a sweet-natured farmer from Kentucky who looked like a linebacker crossed with a Humvee.

'Tabi, that's not fair to ask,' said Jonathan. 'A man should never comment on a woman's size. And stop calling him Bagpipes, you insane Greek woman.'

'Thor likes it,' she threw back. 'Look at that smirk. He could use a little lightening up. And I happen to excel at that activity. Dive in, Nessie, we won't bite. I see you. I have too many male friends not to have your number. Stop hating people.'

Rory grunted. He didn't hate people. He was simply ambivalent about most of them.

'So, you're Scottish?' Sabrina asked, brightly.

He nodded.

She frowned. 'Where's your kilt then?'

'He's in disguise,' Ben laughed.

'But he's probably got some shortbread in his pockets,' added Tristan.

'Do you?' Sabrina asked, hopefully.

Rory shook his head.

'Where do you live in Scotland?' she continued.

'The Highlands.'

'Ooh! Do you live in a castle?' Sabrina sat up straighter, sloshing wine onto her hand. She moved to lick it off, and Rory gently took the glass before she tipped the contents over herself.

'I think he's the secret star of a reality show in Scotland about living in caves,' said Tabi.

Rory allowed himself a small smile. Tabi's humour and energy were scarily similar to his wife's. The two of them could never meet. It would be more dangerous than the Large Hadron Collider malfunctioning.

'I live in a cabin,' he volunteered.

Sabrina shuddered. 'I can't think of anything worse.'

'I don't know,' said Tristan. 'Decaf coffee? Vegan bacon? Childbirth?'

Sabrina grabbed her wine from Rory and downed what was left. 'I'd take fake coffee with a side order of fake bacon any day over having kids.'

'You're against kids as a whole or having them yourself?' asked Ben.

Sabrina sighed and held out her glass for Tabi to refill. 'They're okay in small doses. I mean, I've got nieces I adore. But I love walking away from them even more. I'm not sure I'm on the family path. I should want them more than having freedom to do what I like.'

'And that is?' Tristan asked.

Sabrina flailed her arms and Rory ducked to avoid the impact. She was like a cheerleader crossed with a balloon when you let the air out – enthusiastic, but all over the place.

'I want to travel. My mom gave up her whole world to raise

5

us. I don't want that for me. And now my sisters have families and kids, they're chained down. They don't get to do the kinds of things I want to. I don't want to give up on my dreams.' She tipped her glass in Tabi's direction. 'You get me, Tabi?'

'Gotcha,' Tabi replied. 'The kids I know are a pain in the ass.' She looked down at her wine. 'Kids are a pain in the ass,' she muttered.

'I want a pile of kids,' said Jonathan. 'Cheap farm labour. Kidding! I just can't wait to be a dad.'

'You like everyone and everything,' Tabi replied. 'Your best friend is a goddamn pig you couldn't even take to market.'

He shrugged. 'Squeakers is the best.'

'Take it from me,' Tabi continued, 'pregnancy's a drag and kids wreck your life.'

'You've got kids?' Sabrina asked.

'Hell no, but all my best friends do. My friend Elle is like, always pregnant, currently with freaking twins and has another small child. David had an accidental baby, which might end up ruining the best thing that ever happened to him. And my sister-in-law, Bax's sister, and her partner got pregnant immediately with IVF. Like, first try. What I loved about living in Sonoma is now. We now traipse around to kiddie parties, not good parties. Just balloons and Mary's pizza. We're a travelling circus instead of a tribe.'

'I really want children,' said Jonathan. 'I want my own football team.' His brow furrowed. 'But Tanya is undecided.'

'I'd like kids one day,' said Ben. 'I'm one of five so the chaos feels normal.' He turned to Tristan. 'How about you? So far the only people here who want children are the ones who can't actually create them.'

Tristan smiled. 'I don't know. It's a huge responsibility, so I'd want to make sure I did it right.'

'Hmm,' Tabi began. 'Do we need to have a talk about the birds and the bees?'

'Ha ha,' he replied. 'I mean I want to make sure I have them with the right person and that I'd be a good dad.'

'And what about you, Rory?' Tabi asked. 'Fancy a baby haggis?'

Rory's stomach clenched. He'd never seen himself as a father. His upbringing had seen to that. But Zoe wanted a baby, so they'd been trying for one since their wedding, five months ago. He cleared his throat, and everyone leaned forward.

'Not really,' he said. 'But I'll do whatever my wife wants. Whatever makes her happy.'

'Good answer,' Tabi replied.

APRIL

Rory was pretty sure he knew how babies were made, but he'd never expected it to involve holding his naked wife upside down by the ankles. He was as strong as the Highlands but wasn't entirely confident he could hold up one hundred and forty pounds of the most precious human in his life for half an hour.

'Are you sure this is necessary?' he asked, biceps bulging as his grip tightened.

Zoe lifted her head, her long red curls swishing across the wooden floor of the cabin.

'Absolutely. It's gravity. Science.'

'I don't want to drop you.'

'You won't,' she answered cheerfully. 'And if this doesn't work then we're going to have sex in the middle of the standing stones.'

'The ones just off the A835?'

'Yup.'

'Why?'

'Well, according to Bra... local legend, they're built over a convergence of ley lines.'

Rory gritted his teeth at the half mention of his mother's new husband. The dowager Countess of Kinloch, and the most buttoned-up person he knew, was now married to Brad Bauer, a Hollywood superstar twelve years her junior and only seven years older than Rory himself. Brad was bonkers and Rory's mother a royal pain in the backside, but thankfully they lived in LA.

'Zoe, those stones were put up by a local farmer a few years ago for *Outlander* obsessed tourists.'

'Really?'

'Yes.'

'Dammit. Okay, I'll ask Fiona if she knows any other good spots. There's a full moon coming up and I want to take advantage of it.'

Rory lifted her onto the bed.

'Hey! It hasn't been half an hour yet.'

He tucked her into his body and nuzzled her cheek. 'Your face is redder than your hair and there are definitely other things we could do to help make a baby.'

She grinned and reached down to his cock. 'Plan B?'

He rolled her onto her back with a growl and she giggled.

'Zoe MacGinley, as far as making babies is concerned, I'm only ever Plan A.'

A COUPLE OF HOURS LATER, RORY WAS ON THE TELEPHONE IN the Kinloch estate office, hiding behind his alter-ego of 'Greg', whilst listening to a five-minute dissertation on flowers. Posing as a member of staff usually made things quicker and easier.

'They must be blue hydrangeas, but not those terrible electric blue ones, they have to be lavender blue as per the colour wheel I emailed. And white heather, not purple as it can't clash. To be honest with you, Greg, I can't be sure of the quality of your computer monitor, so I'm going to courier up the mood boards I've created. The actual boards. Do you appreciate the significance of this?'

Rory ran a hand into his messy blond hair and bit back a sigh. He'd heard the term 'bridezilla' but presumed most men getting married were happy for their only responsibility to be showing up on time. Mr Campbell Monteith, however, was not most men. He ran a successful interior design business in Edinburgh and was marrying an American human rights lawyer and socialite he met in St. Barts. The wedding was going to be featured in magazines throughout the world and if anything was off point it would reflect on the creative ability of the groom. As such, Campbell had morphed into a micromanaging groomzilla who had the estate offices on speed dial. Rory usually left dealing with people to Zoe, but she was on the other line so he was taking one for the team.

'Yes, Mr Monteith. I fully appreciate the significance,' he replied in a thick Scottish accent.

'And I need written confirmation that the earl will be in attendance.'

Rory looked at his wife sitting behind the desk opposite him.

'You believe the earl will be attending your wedding?' he asked loudly.

Zoe glanced at him, a guilty expression on her face, before swivelling her chair to face the wall and continuing her own conversation.

'Yes, Greg. Do you even read your emails?' asked Campbell. 'I appreciate Lord MacGinley is a busy man, but I'd like to speak to him at least once in the next six months.'

And this is why I put on a Scottish accent and call myself Greg, Rory thought, circling the astronomical figure Zoe had scrawled on a piece of paper the last time he suggested they cancel this particular booking.

'I'm sure that can be arranged, Mr Monteith.'

'Good. Make it so, Greg. Make it so.'

Rory finished the conversation with as much politeness as he could muster, then stalked to his wife's desk.

It was time for payback.

Zoe's chair was facing away, her long legs extended and her feet propped on a two-drawer filing cabinet.

He sat on the edge of the desk behind her and put his hands on her shoulders, massaging away the tension created from a half-hour conversation with a new supplier. She leaned back into his touch, her 'hmms' of affirmation directed down the phone morphing into sounds of enjoyment directed at him. He knew her body intimately and every little shudder and noise of pleasure made his cock twitch. Her wild curls were perched on the top of her head, secured in place with a pencil, leaving her neck exposed. He trailed soft kisses from her hairline down to her ear. She shuddered. Smiling, he gently bit the lobe.

'Ahhh! Er! Oh no, um, I thought I saw a mouse. What? No! We don't have any mice in the castle,' she babbled.

Rory ran a hand inside her top, rubbing her hardened nipple through her bra.

'Oh god! Um, it's a spider. I'm so sorry, I have arachnophobia. Can I ring you back in five minutes?'

'Fifteen,' Rory murmured.

'Sorry, I meant five times three.'

He reached inside her bra.

'Fift... Agh! Call you right back!' she cried, ending the call.

Rory turned her chair and lifted her onto his lap. She

wrapped herself around him, her tongue meeting his as she squirmed against his hardness. He wanted to tease her, to torment her for agreeing he would attend some random person's wedding. But now he didn't care anymore. It would be a minor inconvenience in a life now filled with love and happiness, all thanks to his crazy, brilliant, firecracker of a wife.

The phone rang.

It was always ringing.

Zoe pulled away with a whimper. 'I should answer it.'

He ripped the cable out of the wall, silencing it.

'Rory!'

He shrugged and grinned, tugging her T-shirt out of her jeans. 'I'll fix it later.'

'And I forgot I've got a meeting at the bakery with Margaret in ten minutes.'

He pulled her top and bra off and palmed her breasts.

'I'll get you off in five,' he growled.

THAT AFTERNOON, IN A BREAK BETWEEN CALLS, ZOE HAD scheduled a meeting to discuss the 'C' word. Before he met his wife, Rory considered Christmas to be the one day a year he went through the motions if he was with his army unit or gritted his teeth if he was with his mother. However, as the Earl of Kinloch, pimping out his castle to pay the bills, it appeared he needed to be thinking about Christmas the previous Boxing Day.

It didn't help that his wife was a believer. It didn't matter what was associated with the holidays, she believed in it all. Santa, the Nativity, mistletoe, stockings, mulled wine, mince pies, carols and Slade. Everything was up for grabs. She might be humming 'Oh Little Town of Bethlehem' one minute, then 'Merry Christmas Everybody' the next. If this level of commitment – to what he considered a manufactured holiday to celebrate capitalism – was exhibited by one of his friends, he would have thought they were deranged. With Zoe, however, he was grudgingly forced to admit it was endearing.

But if his wife loved Christmas, stationery came a close second. These two obsessions had come together and were currently making sweet, sweet love across one entire wall of the estate office. An A3 calendar from Rymans was too insubstantial for what Zoe needed, so she'd created her own with washi tape, Post-its, Sharpies and stickers. Each time a task included her, she stuck a sticker of an angel next to it. When Rory was needed, she stuck up one of The Grinch.

'So, you can't claim I don't run things by you,' she began.

He raised an eyebrow.

'Which of course is nonsense,' she ploughed on, looking at a point an inch above his head.

He cleared his throat.

'So, I—'she continued.

'The Monteith–Kowalski wedding?' he interrupted.

She grinned. 'Did you see how much they are paying? The profits should cover a staff wage for a year.'

'Yes, I saw. I'm surprised to wake each morning and find you haven't tattooed it on the back of my hand overnight.'

Her expression was too excited at that prospect for comfort. He fixed her with one of his stern looks.

She responded the way she always did, by laughing.

He shook his head with a resigned smile. 'Okay, get on with it. I need to check on the cows at Alasdair's farm.'

'Right! Okay! So, from May every other weekend is booked up with weddings and the rest of the time the castle is open for tourists. It's great, but you know it only just covers wages and we're not yet fully in profit.'

He nodded. The busier they became, the more staff were

needed. But wages were the biggest drain on their coffers so the two of them were working seven days a week trying to get everything done and keep costs down.

'This year I want to go all in. We've got the ceilidh, which is free for the village, but I want to have another one for the public and charge for entry.'

That made sense, but Rory knew she was softening him up for a killer blow.

'And we're going to hire out the entire castle to a private party for Christmas week.'

'What private party? Who are they?'

'They're friends of, erm, "He Who Shall Not Be Named".'

'Please tell me he's not going to be there too?'

'No! No, I promise. He's shooting Fight Dragon Club. Your mum assured me they would be staying in LA the whole time.'

Thank god for that. When Rory had visited his mother and new husband he found their lifestyle to be even more irritating and vacuous than he could ever have imagined.

'I want to do a light installation in the castle gardens starting October half-term and running into December,' Zoe continued. 'With wreath-making workshops, mulled wine, carollers et cetera.'

He nodded. It would be an insane amount of work, but these were great ideas. However, his wife had a look he knew all too well and it made the back of his neck tingle.

'What part of "et cetera" involves me?' he asked.

'Erm, you need to grow a beard.'

'Why?' he asked, already fearing the answer.

'I want you to play Santa.'

'Zoe, I'm thirty-five, not sixty-five. Go into The King's Arms and choose someone else. Every night is like a Father Christmas convention there.'

'But they're not the Earl of Kinloch,' she protested.

'Do you think some snot-nosed little kid is going to care?'

Her cheeks were getting redder. This was not a good sign.

'Zoe?'

'We shouldn't be ageist. We need an equal opportunity Santa.'

He closed his eyes and saw exactly what she had in mind.

'So, you're going to advertise a day when all the world and his wife can come and sit on my knee and tell me what they want me to put in their stocking.'

His eyes opened at his wife's howls of laughter.

'Oh my god, Rory, that's genius! "Tell the Earl of Kinloch how you'd like your stocking stuffed". This is amazing! We should do a week of it!'

'One day. And only humans in single digits.'

'What about the oldies? Under ten and over seventy?'

'Are you joking? The pensioners are the bloody worst! Since I carried Mrs McCreedie out of her house last year after the lorry crashed into it, she's been more than a little handsy.'

His wife was now crying with laughter. 'Okay, nine and under, I promise.'

'And do I really need to grow a beard for one day?'

'You need to fully embrace the spirit of Christmas,' she said, wiping her eyes. 'And besides, maybe if we're lucky you can play Joseph to my Mary?'

He drew her into his arms. 'If that's what you want.'

'I always wanted to play Mary in the nativity at school,' she murmured into his chest. 'But I was always a sheep. Or a giraffe.'

'A giraffe?'

'Because I was tall. At least I never had to play the octopus.'

'Huh?

'Vital part of every modern-day nativity. You've gotta move with the times.'

'Humph.'

They stood in silence.

'What if it doesn't happen?' she asked, quietly. 'What if we can't have a baby?'

He held her a little tighter. 'It will. We just need to give it a bit more time.'

She looked at him. 'Do you think we should book in for some tests?'

Her expression broke his heart. He forced a smile.

'Whatever you want. I'm here for you.'

2

APRIL

Two days later Zoe took a break from admin and strolled through Kinloch to a modern housing estate on the edge of the village, where her friend, Fiona, lived with her family. As a child, Zoe had spent a summer in Kinloch and met Fiona for the first time. They were the same age and shared the same sense of humour. Now, two decades on, Zoe was back for good and Fiona had become one of her closest friends.

As the front door opened, an auburn-haired toddler barrelled out, his arms outstretched.

'Dohee! Dohee!'

Zoe lifted him. 'Hey, Liam, you gorgeous little monkey. How goes it?'

A plastic car was thrust in her face. 'Brrrrrrrrmmm! Brrrrrrrrrmmm!' he replied, splattering her face with saliva.

Fiona grabbed her son. 'No brum brum in people's faces, Mister, or Dohee won't ever come back.' She pulled a face at

Zoe. 'Sorry about that. Try and think of it as strengthening your immune system. Come on through and I'll put the kettle on.'

Inside, Zoe sat at the kitchen table with Liam next to her in his high chair as her friend bustled about. Zoe tried to keep her eyes on Fiona's face but her gaze kept falling to her rounded belly. Would *she* ever get pregnant? Zoe had always wanted to be a mother. Now she'd met Rory it was all she seemed to think about. Well, that and jumping him at every opportunity. She kept expecting their first flush of passion to fade but it only seemed to be getting stronger. If the amount of sex correlated with the ability to get pregnant, she should have been carrying octuplets well over a year ago.

'Milk?' Fiona asked, startling her out of her daydreams.

'Yeah, thanks. Ooh! And you've got choccy bickies, too.'

'Bickie! Bickie!'

Fiona broke a biscuit in half and handed it to Liam who stuffed it in his mouth sideways.

'Jesus wept, love, not like that!' Fiona retrieved it and broke it in half again. 'Honestly, Zo, he loves these. I left the room to pee yesterday and came back to find he'd dragged a chair to the counter and was trying to climb up to get to the cupboard. Sneaky little bugger.'

'Bugga! Bugga! Bugga!' yelled Liam excitedly.

'Fuck's sake! I keep forgetting he can talk.'

'Ucks ay! Ucks ay, Mummy!'

Zoe snorted with laughter, which set Liam off even more. Fiona attempted to be stern with her son, but he seemed to know from her expression that this word would get the maximum reaction from the most important person in his life.

'Just wait till your father gets home, Mister,' said Fiona, wagging her finger at her son.

Fiona's husband, Duncan, worked as an electrician and rope

access specialist on oil rigs in the North Sea and was away two weeks out of every four.

'How's it going?' Zoe asked.

Fiona's hand went to her bump. Zoe knew how anxious she was each time her husband left. Her mum, Morag, had been pregnant with Fiona's younger brother, Jamie, when her father had died on the rigs doing the same job that her husband now did. Fiona usually tried to hide her concern but now the smiles about Liam's antics slipped away.

'Not great to be honest, Zo.' She rubbed at a spot on the table. 'With the state of the world, half the crew doesn't know if they'll be laid off tomorrow then reinstated the week later. He's fed up with the uncertainty.'

Zoe gave her friend's hand a squeeze.

'You must be sick of me moaning by now,' Fiona grimaced.

'No! Of course not. Complain all you like. That's what friends are for.'

'It's like we've made a pact with the devil. The money's so good we can afford to buy our forever home. But I don't know how I'm going to cope once the new baby comes.'

'Babyyyyy,' repeated Liam, solemnly.

Zoe understood. One child looked hard enough but having to be a single mum half the time with a newborn as well didn't sound much fun.

'You know you can always ask me to help?'

'Zo, you're so busy it's a miracle I see you at all.'

Zoe sighed. Fiona was right. She'd come to Scotland looking for a quieter life but had ended up the Countess of Kinloch, married to Thor's overly libidinous brother and fifty per cent responsible for a castle and thousands of acres of land. Something was going to have to give. She took a gulp of tea.

'Fi, is the milk off?'

'Fresh this morning.' Fiona sipped hers. 'Tastes okay to me.'

Zoe took another mouthful. 'It tastes weird.'

'Decaf teabags?'

'Nah, I've been drinking decaf here for the last six months.'

'Zoeeeeeeee...' Fiona drew out the last syllable, her eyes sparkling.

She shook her head. 'I can't be. I tested negative again this morning.'

'Are you late?' Fiona asked.

'Four days, but that's normal. You know my cycles are all over the place.'

Fiona leaned back in her chair and pulled a pregnancy test out of a low drawer, placing it on the table.

'You could do another one?'

Zoe shrugged. 'It'll still be negative. They always are.'

'Well then you'd know?'

'I don't know, Fi.'

'Zoe, Zoe, Zoe, Zoe,' Fiona chanted, getting louder and louder.

'Dohee! Dohee! Dohee!' yelled Liam.

'Alright, alright!' She laughed. 'I'll go pee on a stick.'

A minute later she was back and laid the test face down on a wad of toilet paper. Fiona set the timer on the oven, and they waited. Even Liam was silent, his eyes flicking between them as he tried to figure out what was going on.

The beep of the oven went through Zoe with a crack of adrenaline. Every time was the same. The nervous hope, the flash-forwards to possible futures, then the deflating disappointment at the sight of only one blue line.

'Go on then, look,' Fiona urged.

Zoe flipped it over as if she wasn't bothered and stared at two blue lines. She blinked. Was it true? Was she *really* pregnant? She looked in astonishment at Fiona's shocked face.

'Well, bugger me, Zo.' Fiona exhaled. 'You're going to have a baby.'

'Bugga mee! Bugga mee! Babyyyyyyy!' agreed Liam.

⊶❦⊷

RORY'S FOREHEAD WAS DAMP WITH SWEAT, HIS HEART racing.

'Come on, Zoe, push, lass!' Alasdair yelled.

The sounds of her pain echoed around them. Things were not going well.

'Rory, talk to her. I'm going in again.'

Rory stroked her long red curls from her eyes. They were wide and panicked, her breath hot and fast against his face.

'It's okay,' he said. 'Listen to my voice. It's okay.'

Zoe bellowed with pain, the sound nearly knocking him off his feet.

'I've got a foot!' called Alasdair. 'Get the rope! Quick!'

Rory grabbed it and looped it around the protruding leg. It was wet and smeared with blood. Zoe cried out again and his heart lurched.

'Now pull!'

Rory pulled and Alasdair's gloved arm disappeared back into Zoe, emerging with another leg.

'We've got him! Come on, Rory!'

They heaved and the baby slithered out onto the floor. It had curly red hair, just like its mother. Alasdair cleaned its face, and they rubbed the body until it took a few breaths. Rory felt like he'd been holding his for hours.

'Well done,' said Alasdair, patting him on the back. 'I don't think that would have ended well for either of them if you hadn't been here.'

Zoe was now licking her baby, looking far less traumatised than Rory felt. He looked at his bloodied hands.

'Alasdair,' he began, his voice scratchy and low.

'Yes, lad?'

'Why did you have to call her Zoe?'

Alasdair's brow furrowed as if Rory had just asked him to explain why the sun rose every morning.

'Her hair, of course. Never seen a hairy coo with curlier. Do you want to name the calf? He's going to be a strapping wee fella, I just know.'

Rory shook his head. He'd been in life-or-death situations more times than he could remember, but nothing ever quite like this. He heard a vehicle pulling up in the yard outside.

'Finally!' said Alasdair. 'That should be the vet.' He pushed to his feet. 'Oh, I've got the perfect name – I bet he makes the cover of *The Highland Times*.'

Rory's heart sank at Alasdair's excited face.

'I'm going to call him Brad!'

DRIVING BACK TOWARDS KINLOCH AND A RELIABLE PHONE connection, Rory's phone buzzed repeatedly with notifications. Was something wrong? He glanced at the screen. Most of the messages were from Zoe, asking after her cow and wanting to know when Rory was coming back. He pulled into the back courtyard of the castle and cut the engine. This was the first birth he'd attended that had been touch and go. Was that what human birth was like? Was this what Zoe was going to have to experience if they ever got pregnant? He ran his hands into his hair, tugging at the roots. He wanted to talk it out but didn't want to share these fears with Zoe and freak her out. Would his best mate, Charlie, understand?

A text came through.

TABI: Yo, Bigfoot. Something's been plucking at Yia Yia's third eye telling her I need to check in with you. You okay?

How had he ended up with a loud-mouthed American winemaker for a friend? And was he okay? He rubbed his face. Of course he was.

Inside, Zoe ended her call abruptly when he came in.

'Roryyyyyyyy!' She ran to his side and threw her arms around his neck. 'I love you, I love you, I love you, I LOVE YOU!'

He grinned, his heart lifting. They didn't need a baby, they just needed each other.

'I love you too. Always. Sorry I'm late. Zoe had her calf.'

'Eek! Boy or girl?'

'Boy.'

'Called?'

He pulled a face and she laughed. 'Oh my god. Did Alasdair name him after you?'

Rory shook his head. 'Think of the worst possible name he could have chosen.'

She affected a look of concentration, but he knew she'd guessed the name by the sparkle in her eyes.

'Arnold? After my dad?'

He shook his head again.

'Stuart? After yours?'

'No.'

'Um, was the calf named after your step-fa—'

He growled in warning.

She shrieked with laughter. 'I bet Alasdair thinks it'll get him on the cover of *The Times* or Brad's Instagram feed. God, people are nuts. You know the last three boys born in Kinloch were all called Bradley?'

He nodded.

'They should have been christened Rory,' she continued.' That's a far better name.'

She kissed him and all his cares melted away.

'Your stubble feels funny.'

'I can shave it off.'

'December 26th. You can be like a sheep and have an annual shearing.'

He rolled his eyes as he grinned at her. She was a lunatic, but she was *his* lunatic. She pulled away and went to her desk.

'Close your eyes,' she instructed. 'And hold out your hands.'

'Have I forgotten my birthday again?'

'Nope. Stay still.'

Something light was placed in his palm.

'Okay, you can open them now.'

He did, looking first at her face, then at the white stick in his hand.

'I'm pregnant!' Zoe screamed. 'We're having a baby!'

3

APRIL

Breathe in, two, three, four, and hold, two, three, four. Breathe out, two, three, four...

Rory's jaw clenched tight as he did the breathing exercise Zoe's best friend, Sam, had once talked about. Sam said it calmed her down when she was stressed. Right now, with Zoe curled up on his lap on the phone to her mother, he needed all the help he could get to hide his emotions. He was absolutely terrified.

'I don't feel pregnant. Should I feel pregnant? What am I meant to be feeling? Oh my god, Mum, I'm pregnant!'

Zoe's mother, Mary, was on speakerphone and her laugh was warm.

'My darling girl, you won't feel anything for weeks but you might get very tired and nauseous. You need to rest.'

'But I don't want to! I've got to get everything organised for Christmas.'

Oh god. Fucking Christmas. Rory's heart rate spiked as he tried to work out when Zoe might give birth. *December? January?*

'Zoe love, it's the beginning of April,' said her mother.

'Yes, but I'm due mid-January so what if the baby comes early? I can't leave anything to chance. Or to The Grinch.'

'Rory, are you listening to this slander?'

He let his breath go. He had to get it together.

'Yes, Mary,' he replied. 'Although if you weren't on the other end of the phone I would have already tuned out.'

'Oi!' said Zoe, wiggling the fingers of her free hand. 'I know how ticklish you are. These digits are deadly weapons and I'm not afraid to use them.'

He flinched. The thought of being tickled was almost enough to displace the fear that his wife was finally pregnant. 'Apologies, Mary. What I meant to say is that I am tuned one hundred per cent to Radio Zoe and hanging on her every word.'

'Oh dear.' Her mother laughed. 'That's your first mistake. If I paid attention to half of what Arnold said I'd go mad or fall asleep.'

'Mum! This is serious! Christmas is serious! I've got to be prepared.'

Breathe in, two, three, four, and hold, two, three, four. Breathe out, two, three, four, and hold, two, three, four. Rory's brain stumbled forward through the year. Sod Christmas preparations. What about preparing the cabin for the baby? In the army, he'd been trained to assess every environment for risks and right now, thinking about splinters from the floor, burns from the Rayburn, slips in the bathroom and falls from the furniture, the cabin was looking more dangerous than a temple trap from an *Indiana Jones* movie.

'Darling,' Mary continued. 'I had to be induced with you at forty-two weeks and most first-time mums give birth ten days after they're supposed to. You'll be fine. This is going to be your last quiet Christmas for quite a while, so you need to enjoy it.'

Breathe in, two, three, four, and hold, two, three, four. Breathe out...

'When does Dad get home? Does he have his mobile on him? I want you to tell him the moment he gets in.'

'He left it at home again. He'll be back about seven, just as I'm heading out to choir practice. Will you still be at the castle?'

'No, we'll be home by then. Tell him to take his phone tomorrow and I'll ring him in the morning.'

'Okay, love, will do. Now rest up and let your wonderful husband take care of you.'

Yes. This was something he knew he could do. As she said goodbye to her mother, she shifted in his lap.

'Rory...'

'Hmmm?'

'I think I need to lie down.'

Panic flared. 'Are you okay?'

She giggled at his response and guided his hands under her top to her breasts. 'I need you to take care of me.'

Relief flooded through him. They were back on solid ground. She arched into his touch, gyrating on his thickening cock. He brushed his lips against her throat and she shivered.

'Well, we'd better get you home then,' he murmured.

THERE WAS NOTHING MORE INTOXICATING TO RORY THAN getting his wife off. Over and over again. His own orgasms were always spectacular and carried a risk of aneurysm, but the sensation was deeper and more complex with Zoe. The taste of her on his tongue, the feel of her fevered skin, the way her thighs clamped around his head, the sound of her screaming his name. It was a rush like no other. And now, making her come was the ultimate distraction from the baby elephant in his mental room. However, if making her come was the source of his greatest pleasure, being interrupted whilst doing so was the source of his greatest displeasure.

Bang! Bang! Bang!

'Rory,' she gasped. 'There's someone at the—'

He flicked his tongue faster. Her thighs were trembling. She was so close. Unless the cabin was on fire he wasn't going to stop.

'Hang on!' Zoe cried to whoever was outside. 'I'm commmm-mmmmmmmmminnnngggggggg!'

Her body stiffened and he held her tightly, licking harder, pushing the wave of her orgasm faster through her till her body convulsed on the bed.

'Oh my god, oh my god, oh my god,' she gasped.

When her body went limp, he gently pulled away and covered her with the duvet. He was still dressed, so adjusted his cock for decency, stalked to the door and opened it a crack.

'Fiona, is everything okay?'

'It is now. Ish,' she replied. 'Congratulations by the way. Is your mum pleased?'

'She doesn't know. We only told Zoe's parents.'

'Well, they must have accidentally let the cat out of the bag, or the bun out of the oven.' She passed him her phone. 'Don't panic, it's gone now. This is just a screenshot.'

Rory stared at Brad's face on his Instagram feed. He looked deranged with excitement. The caption across the bottom screamed: 'I'm going to be a Pop Pop!!!'

What. The. Fuck.

'Luckily Sam saw it pretty much the moment it was posted and called me. I told her Zoe was about ten seconds pregnant and hadn't told anyone yet. So, Sam phoned Brad and made him take it down. We think it was only up about ten minutes.'

He felt Zoe behind him.

'What's going on?' she asked.

He handed her the phone. 'It's been deleted now.'

'Oh god.' Her hand went to her stomach. 'But only Mum knows! And I told her not to tell anyone.'

'Your dad must have accidentally said something.'

Her eyes welled up. 'I wanted this to be a secret. Something just for us. Even if only for a little while.'

He pulled her into his arms. 'I know.'

'And the first three months are the most...' she broke off as if she couldn't say what they were all thinking.

Rory turned to Fiona. 'You okay to stay with Zoe for twenty minutes while I drive up the hill and attempt to murder my mother's husband with only the power of my voice?'

Fiona grinned. 'Yep, no worries.'

'Will you phone my dad too?' Zoe asked. 'If it was him he's going to be devastated.'

He kissed the top of her head. 'Of course. He hasn't done anything wrong.'

Zoe frowned. 'Be nice to Brad. He's just excited, that's all. He doesn't mean any harm.'

His response was a harrumph. He wasn't going to make any promises he couldn't keep.

RORY PULLED INTO A LAYBY WHERE THEY COULD ALWAYS find reception. He was perfectly happy insulated from the rest of the world with Zoe at the cabin, but if something happened to her or the baby, the lack of phone signal wasn't practical. He rubbed his stubble and sighed. Things were going to change whether he wanted them to or not.

He took a deep breath and rang his mother's number in LA.

'Why didn't you tell me?' she demanded the moment the call connected.

'That's what you're leading with?'

'Is that Rory?' he heard Brad in the background. 'Can I speak to him, I need to—'

'Bradley!' his mother barked.

'Yes, Countess,' he replied instantly. The sound was muffled as if Barbara was holding the phone to her chest, but Brad's obedient tone reminded Rory of his army days.

'Go to the room.'

Huh?

'Yes, Countess.'

What the actual...?

Rory heard his mother's heels clicking across the floor, then the sound of a door closing.

She sighed. 'Rory, I want to apologise on behalf of my husband. I was out and Bradley rang Arnold to chat about fishing. Arnold thought we knew, and Bradley became overly excited about becoming a...' – she cleared her throat – 'about your pregnancy and wanted to share that excitement with the world.'

Rory paused and looked out of the truck window. Apologies were so rare from his mother he half expected to see a sounder of pigs soaring across the glen.

'I wish you'd told me first,' she continued, 'so I could have handled him appropriately.'

'Mum. We only found out this afternoon.'

'Well, we're very happy for you, dear, and looking forward to helping you run this pregnancy properly.'

'What?' Growing up, he remembered his mother being about as maternal as a cuckoo. Was she about to morph into Mary Poppins? 'What is there to run?' he asked. 'Zoe's growing a baby.'

His mother laughed. 'My dear boy. Any fool can have a baby. Your wife is gestating the future Earl of Kinloch.'

Rory pinched the bridge of his nose. Once again, he wished he was just a simple carpenter.

'Mother. There's a fifty per cent chance it will be a girl.'

Barbara sniffed. 'And, of course, that scenario would be delightful. Every child is a blessing.'

He rolled his eyes.

'So,' she continued, 'we'll have a press release drafted for you in the next few hours and I'll start compiling lists of the best doctors and researching the correct name. Tell Zoe not to worry about a thing. She needs to rest. I can take care of it all.'

'Mum—'

'You must give Zoe my fondest regards. I know I may not sound it, Rory, but I'm extremely excited. Not in the same way as Bradley of course – I'm not American – but I'm thrilled for you all the same and looking forward to being a grandmother—'

'Mum—'

'Good grief! That makes me sound old. Thank goodness Honey Boo-Boo is arriving in an hour for my personal training session. She may have an absolutely ridiculous name, but she nearly beat Bradley at arm wrestling. An extraordinary woman.'

'Mum! You need to back off and give Zoe some space. One in four pregnancies doesn't even make it past three months.'

There was a pause.

'That's true, although he's half MacGinley, so stronger than the common herd.'

'Jesus Christ! Zoe's stronger than I am and you know it.'

Barbara sighed. 'Well, she'd better be. Birthing you was a challenge and now look at the size of you. Unless you elect for a caesarean section, your wife will be attempting to deliver an ox.'

4

MAY
Six weeks + two

For the two weeks since finding out his wife was pregnant, Rory kept his operating system set to non-baby status. Zoe didn't look pregnant and told him she didn't feel any different. Therefore, she wasn't really going to give birth in eight months and his life could continue contentedly on.

That was until they were driving down the side of the glen towards the cabin and Zoe stiffened.

'Stop the truck!'

He screeched to a halt at the side of the road, and she threw herself out, bending over and breathing heavily. By the time he reached her, Bandit was already at her side, rubbing against her leg.

Rory tentatively stroked her back. 'Are you okay? Do you think you're going to be sick?'

Hands braced on her thighs, she was breathing slowly in

through her nose and out through her mouth. Anxiety squeezed his chest.

'I don't think so. It just came on so quickly.'

She's alright. Get it together. 'How do you feel now?'

She cranked herself vertical and he examined her face.

She giggled and ran her fingers over his frown lines. 'I'm fine. I'm sure it's just a one-off. You took that last bend too fast and left my tummy behind. I think I should drive the rest of the way.'

The relief was so palpable he thought he might float away. *She's okay. Everything's okay.*

He raised an eyebrow. 'You think you're a safer driver than me?'

'I never said I was *safer*. Being driven by me is more exciting. Therefore, I'm a *better* driver than you.'

God, how he loved her. He tried to keep his face stern but could feel the corners of his mouth twitching.

'I prefer the term "terrifying",' he replied. 'When you're at the wheel it's like playing chicken with death.'

She grinned. 'And doesn't it make you feel alive? You're living in the moment. It's like mindfulness training. Very Buddhist. I'm basically a spiritual guru.'

He leaned down, his lips almost touching hers. 'Well,' he murmured, 'I do like worshipping you.'

Her breath hitched. 'Do you, er, fancy entering my temple?'

He tugged her closer, the hard length of his cock pressing into her belly.

'Yes, I do,' he replied. 'Many, many times.'

RORY HAD HOPED THE NAUSEA WAS A ONE-OFF, BUT OVER THE next twenty-four hours he knew it was here to stay.

'I thought it was meant to be morning sickness, not

evening sickness,' Zoe grumbled as she lay on the sofa, Basil, her pet Dumbo rat sniffing her hand and Bandit at her feet on the floor.

Their animals seemed to know instinctively that something was different and wanted to stay close to her at all times. Bandit, in particular, was being extra protective, and Rory had to put him outside whenever they had sex in case the dog thought Zoe was in pain. The last thing he wanted was having his bollocks bitten off.

'You always like to buck the trend,' he replied as he fed the Rayburn more wood. 'Are you sure I can't persuade you to eat something?'

She pulled a face. 'The thought of food makes me feel sick. The only thing I like the look of right now is you, but that's not going to sustain me for the next seven and a half months.'

'Oh, I don't know. Apparently—'

She threw a sofa cushion at him. 'Don't even go there, Rory MacGinley.'

He opened a cupboard and retrieved a tube of Pringles. His diet may have consisted of water, salt and beef from the estate herd, but Zoe was now living off crisps, smoked salmon and pickled gherkins.

She perked up. 'Ooh! Prawn cocktail flavour.'

Ten minutes later the tube was empty.

'Thank you for not saying anything,' she said as Basil scouted for crumbs.

'Well, apparently once you pop, you can't stop,' he replied. 'I'm just glad to see you eating.'

She yawned. 'I'm so tired, Rory, and there's too much to do.'

He didn't know how to reply. She was right. He had no idea how they were going to get everything done for Christmas on top of their already insane workload.

'I can make it work,' he told her with as much conviction as he could muster. '*Greg* will have to put in extra hours at the office, that's all.'

'But all my plans. They need sorting now.'

He rubbed his chin. 'Well, the beard is in hand. That's one thing you don't need to worry about.'

'Your beard isn't going to sell Christmas, no matter how impressive it is.'

'I think it's at least worthy of one of your crazy calendar ideas.'

As soon as the words were out of his mouth, Zoe's face lit up and his stomach sank.

'Oh my god, YES! You can do a sexy Santa calendar!'

His head shook so fast, her face was a blur. 'No, no, no, no, no, no fucking way.'

She slumped back onto the sofa. 'Okay,' she grumbled. 'No calendar.'

He knelt on the floor and took her hand. 'Whatever Santa fantasies you have inside your beautifully bonkers head, I promise I will do my best to indulge them. Do you want to cross anything off your wish list tonight?'

She smiled. 'Can I see your north pole?'

He raised an eyebrow. 'Only if I get to lick your baubles.'

JUNE

Nine weeks

Rory was an onion of anxiety. At his core was the deep-rooted belief that he would be a terrible father. He could unpick the thought with logic and common sense, but the unconscious fear still remained that he would, through DNA or imprinting, behave the same way his father had towards him. Built over this were layers upon layers of stress. Would

Zoe be okay? Would she survive labour and birth? Was the baby healthy? How could he take some of her workload away? Even if he managed to rationalise one worry, there was another hiding underneath.

He wanted to talk to his best friend about it all. But Charlie was in LA and their time zones never seemed to match. Rory was also working around the clock to try and keep on top of the everyday running of the estate, all the weddings they had booked and the planning for Christmas.

But for all the weight on his shoulders, he knew he had it easy compared to Zoe. The only time she wasn't exhausted or nauseous was when she was asleep, the brief moments she could eat, or when she was orgasming. Keeping her satisfied was a duty he undertook with absolute dedication.

Right now, she was riding him, and he was trying to keep his own climax at bay until she'd had her third. Her expression had been one of bliss, but her closed eyes were twitching in a way that worried him.

He squeezed her thighs. 'You okay?'

Her eyes snapped open. 'Yes, I'm fine.' She moved faster but was now biting her lower lip.

'Zoe, stop! Are you sure you're alright?'

She got off him and sat on the bed cross-legged, holding her stomach. He got to his knees, his heart pounding.

'I don't know,' she said. 'My tummy hurts, that's all.'

'What can I do? Hot water bottle? Cup of tea? Should I go up the hill and ring the midwife?'

Her face was pale. 'No, I'm fine. It's nothing.'

'Are you—'

'No, no, no, no, no!'

Fuck! 'What's wrong?'

She leapt off the bed and ran for the bathroom, leaving a puddle of blood behind on the sheet. It was huge.

Fear strangled him, turning his vision white. He stumbled off the bed and followed her, blood roaring in his head. He had to hold it together for her, even though he was being torn apart.

She was sitting on the toilet, her hands clasped in her lap, rocking back and forth.

He knelt by her side. 'What can I do? Shall we go to the hospital?'

She was shivering. 'Can you clean the bed?' she whispered. 'I don't want to see it.'

He nodded and dashed out. He had to deal with her shock first, so returned to drape a blanket over her shoulders and help her feet into fluffy slippers. She murmured something and he crouched down.

'What did you say, love?'

'It's common to bleed during pregnancy. I'm sure everything's fine.'

'I know it is,' he replied, not believing a word he was saying. 'Can I get you anything else before I deal with the sheets?'

She shook her head.

He closed the bathroom door behind him and stared at the bed. There was bleeding during pregnancy, then there was this. He'd seen blood before, and he'd seen death. But nothing had ever felt like this. His heart was being ripped to shreds.

He had done this.

He had hurt the love of his life, and most likely cost her the thing she wanted more than anything else in the world.

He clenched his jaw against the rising tide of nausea. *Breathe in, two, three, four...*

He pulled the sheet off the bed. The blood had soaked through to the woollen mattress protector. He dragged it off.

The stain continued as if burrowing its way to the centre of his soul.

How could he ever forgive himself?

He chucked the linen in a bucket of cold water and scrubbed at the mattress the best he could, then rushed back to check on her.

'How are you doing?'

She shrugged. Her cheeks were dry, and somehow that made it even worse.

'I don't want to leave you, but I should call the midwife, see what they say?'

She nodded. 'Yes please.'

'I'll be as quick as I can.'

He pulled some pads out of the cabinet and put them on the side. 'I'll just grab you some water and some painkillers.'

The nod of her head was almost imperceptible.

He returned with a glass, a packet of paracetamol, and a sleepy Basil who he placed in her hands.

'I know he's not as handsome as me, but he's probably better at looking after you.'

She tried to smile but her lower lip was wobbling.

He wanted to stay but knew he needed to speak to a professional. He kissed the top of her head.

'I love you, Zoe. It's going to be okay. I promise.'

NINE WEEKS + ONE

Zoe passed more blood overnight. Rory held her when she managed to nod off, then changed her pad when she woke up. She didn't want to look at it and he understood. Until they knew for sure what had happened, he wanted her to believe it was all okay. Despite how much he rationalised it, he couldn't believe there was still a baby there. The midwife had made an appointment for them at EPAU, the Early Pregnancy Assessment Unit, so they set off early that morning for Raigmore hospital.

'I don't feel sick anymore,' she said quietly after they'd been driving for a few minutes.

His hands gripped the steering wheel tighter as he tried to keep his voice calm. 'That could just be adrenaline?'

'I don't know. I just keep waiting to feel like I did yesterday, but I don't.'

'Let's see what they say, eh?'

Tears ran silently down her cheeks. 'I think it's clear what they're going to say.'

He reached over to clasp her hand in his. He had no idea how to make this right, but he was going to die trying.

THE WAITING ROOM WAS FILLED WITH MISERABLE-LOOKING couples who avoided eye contact. Rory gave their details to the receptionist, then they waited, Zoe sitting on his lap, her tears wetting the front of his shirt.

'Mrs MacGinley?'

This was it. Schrodinger's baby. Their child was there and not there. Both realities existed until confirmed either way. He took her hand and they entered the consulting room.

Inside, Zoe told the nurse and sonographer what happened.

'Do you know if you passed the embryo?' the nurse asked.

She shook her head. 'Not yet.'

'Okay, we're going to do a transvaginal ultrasound and see what's going on, okay?'

She nodded.

'If you can take your bottoms off, we can take a look.'

The sonographer applied a strip of lube to what looked like a dildo.

What the fuck?

Rory cleared his throat. 'Erm, is that, er, safe?'

The woman smiled, knowingly. 'That's what all the husbands ask. It may be bigger than what you're used to seeing, but I assure you it's perfectly safe. And it's only going in a couple of inches.'

Breathe in, two, three, four, and hold, two, three, four...

He clasped Zoe's hand as she lay back. This was the moment they confirmed what he already knew.

'Okay, let's take a wee look, shall we?'

His heart was thudding inside his chest. Tears ran down the sides of Zoe's face and he gently wiped them away, feeling them as his own.

'So, if you look on the screen, you can see your baby there.'

'I know,' said Zoe. 'I haven't passed it yet.'

'And there's the heartbeat.'

Rory's grip on her hand tightened. 'What?'

'Your baby's heartbeat. They're doing fine and dandy.'

Zoe sobbed and he hugged her into his chest. 'It's okay, Zoe. Our baby's okay.'

Our baby. Our baby. Our baby. The words bounced around inside his head. There was a future child inside her, and he'd nearly killed it.

The woman removed the probe and handed Zoe a wad of paper towels.

'You can put your clothes back on now.'

Zoe was still crying so much that her body was clumsy, so he helped her dress. She sat on his lap, and he curled his arms protectively around her.

'Why did this happen?' he asked the sonographer, needing to hear from them if it was his fault.

'Well, did you know, Zoe, that you have a bicornuate uterus?'

'A what?' she asked.

'It's heart shaped. About four in a thousand women have them. Baby MacGinley is implanted on one side, but the other doesn't have anything in it so thinks you are due a period. This is what caused the bleeding. It's likely it will keep going for a while so don't be too concerned.'

'What does this mean for the pregnancy?' she asked.

'It's still early days so difficult to say. Some women do have issues such as preterm or breech babies, but others go through life never knowing they have this condition.'

Still early days. Issues. Preterm. Breech.

He'd done this to her, and he could do it again.

Zoe wanted to speak to her mum, so Rory gave her some privacy and sat her in the hospital cafe with a pot of tea and a slice of cake. He stood just outside under a grey sky, the crushing weight of responsibility pressing down on him. He was used to putting his big feet in situations, but now his big cock had almost lost them their child.

His phone vibrated in his pocket.

TABI: Nessie, Darling. I'm pissed because you're the reason I'm still awake at two in the frikking morning. Yia Yia just called, well my mom did, and Yia Yia won't let it go. Her third eye is still shining on you. Stop giving me all this "I'm fine, go away. Who is this?" shit. If you won't talk to me, I need to know you're talking to someone or Yia Yia won't let me rest. Haggis, pixie, I don't give Basil the rat's ass who you talk to, just do it.

TABI: Or I'm ringing Zoe.

RORY: Don't ring Zoe.

TABI: It speaks! If I'd have known that threat worked so well, I would have used it weeks ago.

RORY: Zoe's nine weeks pregnant and had a bleed. We're at the hospital now.

TABI: Fuck! No. No. One of us has to be able to have kids. Is the baby okay?

RORY: For now.

TABI: I'm so sorry. Tell me you have good doctors. Do you need me to make a call?

RORY: Her uterus is heart shaped, so half of it was trying to have a period. But it's really my fault.

TABI: How d'you figure that out?

RORY: We had sex.

TABI: And you think because you tossed your caber too far, she's doomed?

RORY: The bleed started when we were having sex.

TABI: I hate to break it to you, or any man, but your penis doesn't have magical powers.

TABI: And congratulations! Yes, I know it's early days, but this is amazing news!

RORY: Thanks. Keep it to yourself.

TABI: Can't. Have to tell Yia Yia so she'll shut the fuck up. And I will probably tell Bax, I tell him everything.

RORY: Fine. No one else in your bleeding gigantic circle.

TABI: Where's Zoe now? Have you told her your tremendous scary cock theory?

RORY: She's talking to her mum. And no, she's got enough to deal with without more of my crap.

TABI: She married you. She's used to your crap. Don't keep it in. I'm here. Everything happens for a reason. Even the pain of carrying around your tree trunk of a peen.

RORY RANG CHARLIE. HE DIDN'T CARE WHAT TIME IT WAS in LA.

He picked up just as Rory was expecting it to go to voicemail.

'This had better be good,' Charlie said, his voice gravelly. 'I've got a photoshoot in the morning and need my beauty sleep.'

'I need some advice.'

'Huh? No attempt at a witty comeback? No slagging off *Cosmopolitan's* Sexiest Man of the Year?'

'Not this time.'

There was a pause.

'Fuck, okay. Hang on.'

Rory heard a slapping sound.

'Right,' said Charlie, sounding much more alert. 'I've deployed stage one of waking myself up. How can I help?'

'I'm at the hospital. Zoe's nine weeks pregnant and had a massive bleed last night. The baby's okay, but it's all my fault.'

There was silence, then the sound of Charlie slapping his face again.

'That's a lot to unpack,' he began. 'First up, congrats, knew you had it in you. Second, is Zoe okay? Third, can I tell Valentina? And fourth, how the actual fuck is it your fault?'

Rory's heart felt too heavy for his chest. 'Zoe doesn't have to stay in the hospital and says she's fine, but who really knows? You can tell Valentina, but please keep it from her family or the whole bloody world will know.' He sighed. 'And it's my fault because it happened when we were having sex.'

'Is that what the doctor said?'

'Not in so many words, but Zoe's got a heart-shaped uterus which can make a pregnancy risky. And...'

'Ye-es?'

'You know,' Rory replied, testily, 'I've got a big cock.'

Charlie snorted. 'Not as big as mine, mate.'

'Bollocks.'

'Yep, they're bigger too.'

'Fuck off, this is serious.'

'So, why do you need my advice? Do you need me to hook you up with Hollywood's finest plastic surgeon for a penis reduction?'

'Don't be a twat.'

'Can't help it. It's hardwired into my DNA. And anyway, I think Valentina finds it cute.'

Rory thought about Charlie's fiancée. He was glad his friend had finally found someone who truly loved him.

'You still there?'

'Yeah,' Rory replied. 'I need to ask for your advice.'

'So you said.'

'But I don't want you to laugh or take the piss.'

'Mate, you know I can't promise that.'

'Fine—'

'Hang on. I'll be serious. Come on, out with it.'

Rory sighed. 'Okay, here's the deal. Pregnancy is less fun than five days in a foxhole with food poisoning. Zoe's knackered, feels sick the whole time and the only time she feels okay is when she's asleep, sometimes when she eats, or if she's having an orgasm. There's no fucking way my cock is going anywhere near her until that baby's out, so I need some alternatives.'

'Fuck my life. Your fingers? Your tongue?'

'If I'm involved, then she'll want it all.'

'The earl's sausage as well as the side dishes?'

Rory raised his eyes to the heavens. 'You are such a dick.'

'Yes, but right now the problem is your dick. Have you spoken to Zoe about all this?'

'No.'

'Don't you think you should?'

'I don't want to. She's overwhelmed with being pregnant and her plans for bloody fucking Christmas.'

'Is that the song by The Pogues and Kirsty MacColl?'

Rory ignored him. 'I'm trying to keep it together for her right now. She's the one with the hard job, she doesn't need my bullshit. There's plenty to take me away from the cabin, so I need to get her some, erm, toys...'

'You don't have any already?'

'What? Fuck no.'

'Seriously? Mate, you're missing a trick. They're not competition, they're fun. A rabbit is your friend, not your foe.'

'A rabbit? What the fuck are you on about? I want a vibrator, not another pet.'

Charlie's laugh was so loud, Rory had to hold the phone away from his ear.

'Mate, you're fucking priceless,' Charlie guffawed.

'Look, are you going to help me or not?'

The sound of Charlie slapping himself echoed down the line, and the laughter stopped. 'Ahem. Yes, Mr Charlie Hamilton is here to save the day. Now, let's start with specifications.'

JULY
Twelve weeks + four

Rory hated hospitals. In his life, they were never associated with anything pleasant. During his army days he'd had the misfortune to be blown up in Afghanistan. He was one of the lucky ones, keeping all his limbs as well as his life. But, lying in a hospital bed with too much time to think had taken its toll. He was confident he'd dealt with his PTSD a long time ago, but every time he smelled the mix of cleaning fluid and cabbage, or heard the squeak of rubber shoes on a linoleum floor, forgotten feelings and emotions woke from their graves to stalk him.

But he had to bite the bullet. Zoe was booked in for multiple appointments and he was going to be there for every single one. So far, pregnancy seemed as fun as a never-ending ride on a decrepit rollercoaster after drinking five bottles of Buckfast. Zoe was still feeling sick the whole time, her bladder had the capacity of a teacup, she was perpetually exhausted, and her emotions had more bounce than a bungee cord. Maybe this was why his parents only had him. God only knew how Fiona always appeared so bonny.

Despite his best intentions and how many hours a day he worked to relieve Zoe's workload, she seemed unable to step off the bridge of the good ship Christmas and let him shoulder more of the responsibility. If he had his way, the celebrations would require less input than a pedalo on a boating lake. However, Zoe's version of Christmas was a cruise liner crossed with a container ship. The one good thing was that she hadn't seemed to notice they'd stopped having sex.

Charlie had come through for him with a shopping list of vibrators long enough to stock a sex shop. Rory had no idea there were so many permutations. They vibrated, they pulsed, they had ultrasonic waves, they sucked, they blew, they had two heads, three heads, ears, rattling balls. Some were even remote controlled. He thought he knew what sex involved, but it was clear he was a caveman living in a sci-fi world and hadn't yet got with the programme. He'd ordered a selection that were mainly external, ensuring anything that would be penetrating her was half the size of his cock, then put them through the castle accounts under 'hospitality and entertainment'.

Red-faced, he'd presented them to Zoe one morning, explaining that he wasn't going to be around much. The embarrassment turned into relief when it seemed they were doing the trick. And when he thought she might initiate any intimacy, he made an excuse to leave the cabin. There was no way he was going to let his selfish desires risk her health or the baby's.

However, sitting in the consultation room at the hospital, it appeared his cunning plan had not been entirely effective.

'Everything's alright then?' Zoe asked the elderly midwife.

'Oh yes, dear. You're now into your second trimester. Your baby is fully formed and just needs to cook.'

'So, it's okay to have sex?'

The woman peered at her over the top of her glasses. 'Why, yes, dear. Are you not indulging in marital relations at present?' She looked keenly at Rory as if he was to blame.

'No. My husband refuses to have sex with me.'

What?

'Oh,' replied the midwife. She took her glasses off to give him the full force of her glare. 'And why is that?'

'Um, we do, I mean, er, you do have...' he broke off and pulled the collar of his shirt away from his neck. Why were hospitals always so bloody hot? 'I've, er, ensured that you are, ahem, satisfied.' He concluded, extremely aware of how dissatisfied both his wife and the midwife currently appeared.

Zoe swivelled in her chair to face him. 'Yes, but none of those instances involve you or your penis going anywhere near my body. And anyway, what about your needs?'

'My needs?' What did they have to do with anything?

'Yes, Rory. I want to give you pleasure. I want your cock in—'

He coughed loudly. Jesus Christ, did she not realise Mrs Doubtfire was taking notes?

'We're not going to have sex until after the birth. I don't want to hurt you or the baby,' he replied testily.

'What?' Zoe screeched. 'Is that what all the sex toys are about?'

The midwife chuckled. 'Mr MacGinley, this is a common concern but entirely unfounded. I'm positive your penis is no different from any other man's. Besides, the female vagina can accommodate pretty much anything, and the cervix and mucous plug protect the baby.'

Zoe had a dangerous glint in her eye. 'See, your penis is as average as the next man's.'

'But what about Zoe's bleed three weeks ago? The risk?'

'Mr MacGinley. Your wife stopped passing blood over a week ago, and even if it continued, normal intercourse is perfectly safe. Your penis—'

'Will you *please* stop talking about my penis?' Sweat was trickling down his back. Fucking hell, women could be terrifying. Thank god his mother was on the other side of the Atlantic.

'Maybe,' Zoe replied, crossing her arms. The movement pushed her breasts together. They'd been getting bigger over the last few weeks.

He tore his gaze away and focused on the little old lady who had a naughtier glint in her eye than his wife's.

'Look, are you sure I'm not going to cause any harm?'

'There are no guarantees, Mr MacGinley, but it's extremely unlikely. If you are truly concerned about your penis, I can make you an appointment with the urologist, Doctor Payne?'

Zoe snorted with laughter.

Rory stood, the chair pushing back with a screech. 'That will not be necessary.'

'Marvellous. I'll see you in a few weeks.' She handed Zoe her maternity notes with a wink. 'Have fun, Mrs MacGinley.'

ZOE SKIPPED OUT OF RAIGMORE HOSPITAL, SINGING 'LET'S Talk About Sex' by Salt-N-Pepa. By the time they'd reached the car park, she was body-popping to 'I Want Your Sex' by George Michael. Back in the truck she started crooning 'Let's Get It On' by Marvin Gaye.

Rory rested his head back and sighed. 'Did you enjoy that?'

'Might have done,' she replied, stretching her arms over her head and pushing out her chest. Rory swallowed and tried not to stare at her breasts.

She put her hand on his trousers. His cock was already hard.

'How is your penis?' she asked innocently. 'It feels a bit stiff. Does it need a massage?'

He closed his eyes and groaned. 'Fuck's sake, Zoe.'

'Rory, please can we go home and put your definitely not average cock in my perfectly safe and normal vagina? Pretty, pretty please?'

He sighed. 'If you're sure?'

Her response was to unlace her boots.

'What are you doing?'

'Getting ready. I want to have sex the moment we get home.'

He started the engine and eased out of the space. He could do this.

BY THE TIME THEY TURNED DOWN THE TRACK TO THE CABIN, Zoe was naked from the waist up. However, as they rounded the final bend, Rory suddenly slammed the truck in reverse.

They were not alone.

'Who the fuck was that?' Zoe asked as she hastily got dressed.

'God knows,' he replied. 'But I'd rather they didn't see your spectacular breasts or my "perfectly average penis".'

'Well, whoever they are, let's get rid of them quickly.'

As soon as Zoe was decent, Rory eased the truck back along the track. The car parked outside the cabin was a big black SUV with tinted windows.

No one got out to greet them.

'Dudes!'

Rory had been glad of the sex reprieve but now his heart sank.

There in the distance, walking up the hill from the loch towards them, hand in hand with Bandit at their side, was his mother and her much younger husband, Hollywood superstar, and all round fruit-loop, Brad Bauer.

'Promise you'll behave,' Zoe said.

Rory was silent.

'Rory!' she hissed.

He grunted.

'Rory grumpypants MacGinley. You have less than a minute to get it together. You will smile. You will make pleasant conversation. And you will not lose your shit if Brad calls you—'

'Son!'

Zoe's nails dug into his arm, the pain a welcome distraction. His father, who'd died three years previously, had been a domineering bully, kicking him off to boarding school in England aged seven. Rory was not in the market for a replacement father figure, certainly not one only a few years older than himself who drank smoothies for breakfast with the consistency and colour of something scraped off the bottom of the loch.

Zoe strode forward. 'Barbara, Brad, what an unexpected surprise.'

His mother air-kissed her and Brad stared at her stomach.

'Where is it?' he asked.

'Bradley, dear,' replied his mother with the kind of tone reserved for toddlers. 'We've been over this already. Zoe won't show for at least another month, maybe longer.'

Brad looked disappointed but immediately bounced back, hugging Zoe. 'Babe, we're so excited!'

Rory stalked over and Brad let go of Zoe and grabbed him in a bear hug. 'There you are. Bring it in, man, bring it in.'

Rory patted his back awkwardly until relieved by his mother.

'Congratulations, darling,' she said, leaving a good six inches between her air kiss and his cheek. 'Although I'm not sure what all this is about,' she said, waving at his beard. 'Are you planning to play Joseph in the nativity this year?'

'Zoe wants me to be Santa.'

His mother looked appalled. 'Aren't you a little young? I didn't think you even *liked* the concept of Father Christmas?'

That was true. The idea of a strange man entering his bedroom when he was asleep had given him nightmares as a child.

'I thought it might bring more people in if they knew the earl was in the suit,' said Zoe.

His mother sniffed. 'Very well, although he'll have to work on his fireside manner.'

'Why are you here?' he asked, as pleasantly as he could manage.

'Rory!'

'It's alright, dear,' his mother said to Zoe with a smile. 'I know it's a little unexpected. We just wanted to congratulate you on reaching the second stage of your gestational journey and offer our assistance.'

'How did you know we were in the second trimester?' he asked. Did he need to sweep the cabin for bugs?

'My shaman, dude!' said Brad. 'He's got his third eye on you.'

Fuck's sake. Not another one. 'Shaman?'

'Yeah, Jesus.'

'Christ,' Rory muttered.

'No, man, his surname's de la Cruz.'

'Darling,' Barbara interjected, laying her hand on Brad's arm. 'You really should pronounce his name "Haysuss".'

'But, babe! "Jesus" sounds way sicker.'

'Bradley,' his mother said, in a tone Rory knew was a warning.

'Yes, Countess,' Brad replied, standing to attention.

Fuck my life. They really did have that dynamic going on.

'So!' Zoe said brightly. 'Your shaman?'

'Yeah, man! I met him at an Ayahuasca retreat. He's been watching you for me. That's how we know how far along you are.'

'That,' continued Barbara, 'and some basic mathematics.'

'What else has Jesús said about my pregnancy?' asked Zoe. Her hands had crept protectively over her belly. Rory stepped closer to her side.

'You're having a boy, and I'm going to be at the birth,' Brad replied.

Silence.

'It's a little bracing this afternoon and we have been waiting a while,' said his mother. 'Shall we adjourn inside for a cup of tea?'

THEY SAT ACROSS THE TABLE FROM EACH OTHER. ZOE chatted with his mother, appearing to have made the decision to ignore Brad's proclamation for the insanity it was. Rory, on the other hand, was engaged in a desperate battle to subdue his inner caveman. He thought he'd come to terms with his mother marrying the Hollywood star but imagining Brad present whilst Zoe gave birth made the green mist descend and his caveman Hulk out.

'So, Zoe dear, how are you feeling?'

Considering how much his mother had hated Zoe in the

past, this pleasant side of her was unnerving.

'Still very tired and a bit sick, to be honest, but okay, I suppose? I don't really know what to expect.'

'Well, Bradley and I don't want to tread on your toes, but we are very keen to help in any way, especially with the logistics.'

'Logistics?' Zoe asked.

'Yes, we'll draft the official announcement and handle the press release. I've already provisionally booked a room at the family's private hospital in Edinburgh for the delivery, and I'm thrilled to say I've already researched the correct name for the baby.'

'The name?' Zoe's voice went up a register.

'Of course you won't know the family tradition, but it's terribly complicated. It took me hours with a genealogist to ensure Rory was named correctly. However, Bradley took me to the Scottish Highland Institute of Tartan Excellence in Los Angeles, and they did it on a computer in a matter of minutes.' She took a piece of paper out of her bag and put it on the table in front of them. 'No need to thank me, dear. It was my pleasure.'

They stared at the printout.

'Stuart Uisdan Murdock Oengus,' said Zoe, faintly.

'Yes, but Uisdan is pronounced Ooshdan,' said Barbara. 'And Oengus has more of an "uh" sound, like *fungus*.'

'Barbara Euphemia Grissel Anabald?'

'I know you're carrying the heir,' his mother continued.' But just in case, I've included the correct name for a girl.'

'*Barbara*?'

'Yes, the first-born female is always named after the paternal grandmother.'

There was a short silence, then Zoe started to laugh.

When Zoe was in very stressful situations, she burst into

hysterical laughter. But it wasn't funny to her; it was panicked, painful and uncontrollable.

Rory held her shaking hands in his. 'Look at me. Breathe with me.'

Her whole body was convulsing as she hyperventilated, desperately trying to draw in air.

'Aha, ahaha, ahahahaha!'

'In through your nose, out through your mouth. You're okay.'

Barbara was looking askance at her, Brad with undisguised interest. Rory made a mental note to ensure Zoe's condition never made it into one of his films.

After a minute, she got her breathing back under control.

He passed her a handkerchief.

'Thank you.' She wiped her eyes, blew her nose, then took a long breath in and out.

'Barbara,' she said firmly. 'I'm extremely appreciative of the thought and time that has gone into your research, however the name of our child will be decided by Rory and myself. The fate of Scotland doesn't depend on us following this particular tradition.'

'But—'

'Babe!' said Brad excitedly. 'They can go with Jesus's vision!'

No, we fucking won't.

'Hay*suss*, Bradley, Hay*suss*.'

'It came to him during ceremony,' Brad continued.

Rory squeezed Zoe's hand, trying to reassure her that whatever wind of insanity was about to blow their way, she could close the door on it.

'Rob Roy Macbeth for a dude, or Heather Loch Leary for a dudette!'

'No,' said Rory.

'And I'm going to give birth in Raigmore hospital in Inverness,' added Zoe.

'Very well,' his mother replied, her lips thinning. Rory knew how much of an effort she was making to be nice.

Brad deflated for a moment, then recovered like a puppy distracted by a new toy. 'We got you some books!'

His mother took two books out of her bag and gave them to Zoe.

One had a picture of a baby and was titled 'The New Contented Little Baby Book'. The other had an elaborately illustrated cover with children and animals and was called 'The Nourishing Traditions Book of Baby & Child Care'.

'Bradley's contribution has a more alternative approach to proceedings but, as you said, this is your pregnancy and you must make the right decisions for you.'

Zoe pushed her chair back, her eyes filling with tears as she embraced his mother. 'Thank you, Barbara.'

She looked startled at the sudden affection, patting Zoe stiffly on the back.

'You guys!' cried Brad, enveloping them both in a hug. 'Bring it in!'

Zoe pulled away.

'Bradley!' snapped Barbara.

He sat back.

Barbara got to her feet. 'We'll stay at the castle tonight, then take the jet back tomorrow afternoon. This is just a flying visit to check in with you both.' She paused and fiddled with the clasp on her bag. 'Unfortunately, due to Bradley's commitments, we may not make it back before the birth.'

Brad stood and put his arms around her. 'Babe,' he said, softly.

She gave him a little nod, then lifted her head. 'Bradley, the castle.'

He straightened. 'Yes, Countess.'

JULY
Twelve weeks + five

SABRINA: Zoe's   pregnant???   OMGGGGG!
CONGRATULATIONS!
    TRISTAN: Congratulations!
    BEN: That's amazing news! Can I tell Laurie?

    JONATHAN: Best. Weekend. Ever. Congrats, guys! Juliet is going to be stoked. Well, she doesn't know you, but she loves kids and I'm rambling. I'm so fucking in love with love right now.

    TABI: And apparently it's his.

    SABRINA: Tabi!!!! WTF?

    BEN: Woah, Tab, that's harsh, even for you.

    RORY: It's okay, she already knows.

    SABRINA: SAY WHAT NOW????

    SABRINA: You told Tabi before us?!!!

    RORY: It's her grandmother's fault.

    BEN: Yah Yah?

    JONATHAN: Yeah Yeah?

TRISTAN: A lady in the streets but a freak in the bed.

TABI: Yia Yia!

TRISTAN: PSML.

RORY: And, Ben, you can tell Laurie. My mother's husband wants to announce it to the world like it's the second coming or something.

SABRINA: Is Zoe due at Christmas?

RORY: Mid-Jan.

SABRINA: Do you know what you're having?

TABI: A Scotch egg.

SABRINA: Ha ha, Tab. You know what I mean.

RORY: We have no clue. Everyone else thinks it's a boy because the patriarchy says that's the preferred outcome. We can find out in a couple of months.

TRISTAN: How's Zoe doing?

RORY: Getting there. Still tired, feels sick the whole time, emotional.

SABRINA: Ginger cookies and Pepto Bismol. That's what my sisters lived off.

RORY: So far it's been mainly pickled gherkins, smoked salmon and Pringles.

TABI: My friend Elle lived on popsicles with her twins. The frozen kind, not yours, Loch Ness.

SABRINA: You must give her our love.

RORY: Will do.

SABRINA: And look after her!!!!!!

RORY: Yeah, yeah.

TABI: It's Yia Yia, Bagpipes. Get it right.

RORY: Bugger off, Tab.

ZOE NEVER KNEW HOW FASCINATING A TINY SLEEPING human could be until she met Fiona's daughter. Even though she knew a pregnant belly contained a baby, now Isla was on the other side of her friend's tummy, the whole process seemed completely unreal. Fiona had given birth two days earlier and this was the first time they'd met the latest addition to the Sinclair household. Rory had held Isla as if she was an unstable bomb for thirty seconds, before going outside to play football in the garden with Duncan and Liam.

'I know I probably sound like I'm mental or something, but now she's here it's like part of me doesn't understand where she came from,' Zoe said quietly. 'It's like you've performed some kind of magic trick.'

Fiona smiled. 'I know what you mean. Ten minutes after I squeezed this little munchkin out of my vagina I wondered if the stork had brought her.'

Zoe clenched her thighs together. 'How was it? The birth?'

'It was fine. Much quicker than with Liam. That lasted a week.'

'A week?' Isla stirred. 'Shhhhhh,' Zoe soothed, rocking her gently.

'Yeah,' Fiona continued. 'I was bloody exhausted. I was in and out of Raigmore more times than a sex addict doing the Hokey Cokey.'

'Why didn't they let you stay?'

'Because I wasn't dilated enough and they didn't want to waste a bed. They want you to come in as late as possible.'

'But how will I know when I'm ready?'

Fiona puffed out her cheeks. 'Honestly, Zo, every labour is different. Just don't even think about calling the midwife until it's been a few hours of contractions so regular and hard you think you might pass out.'

'What?'

'Shit! Sorry, love, that sounded fucking awful. It'll be fine. I promise. Just don't go in until you can't hold a conversation. You don't want to do that car journey more than once.'

'I could have a home birth like you did with Isla?'

'You could. It was a million times better than the hospital. But at the same time, I knew what to expect. And when I was pregnant with Liam, I had to think of Duncan. He would have supported me, of course, if I'd wanted a home birth, but I didn't want him silently freaking out. What does Rory think?'

'We haven't discussed it yet. It all seems so far away. I'd like to be at home for most of it at least. Mum had a really long labour with me as well, and I'd rather be in the cabin than in a hospital ward.'

They sat in companionable silence as Isla slept on, listening to the sounds of Duncan playing football with Liam in the back garden.

'He's not going back this time,' said Fiona.

'Duncan?'

Fiona nodded.

'Because of what happened with your dad?'

'Yes. I didn't want to tell you because I didn't want you to worry, but I kept imagining Mum being pregnant with Jamie when Dad died out on the rigs. That level of stress is just not worth it. And anyway, I've really struggled with this pregnancy and don't want to have to deal with two kids on my own two weeks out of four.'

'Are you going to be okay for money?'

'For a while we should be. We've been saving for years so we have enough to upgrade to our forever home and keep ourselves fed for a few months at least. Dunc can always pick up work as an electrician. We'll be fine.'

⚜

OCTOBER

28 weeks

With one look from his wife, Rory knew he was in trouble.

He'd returned to the cabin to find Zoe, naked from the waist down, washing clothes in the sink. It couldn't have been another bleed as she looked mad, not sad.

'What's happened?'

She pointed a soapy finger at him. '*You* happened, Rory.'

'Um.' He racked his brains to try and think what he'd done. 'The toilet?'

Fuck. He'd forgotten to tell her.

'You baby-proofed the bloody loo and didn't tell me! You know I have the bladder control of a small dog after drinking a pint of builder's tea,' she ranted. 'I tried for thirty seconds to work it out, failed, and pissed myself before I could find a bucket.'

'Shit.'

'Luckily it wasn't that, or I'd be even madder.'

'I'm sorry.'

'Rory, our baby isn't going to be born till next year and won't be mobile for at least six months after that. You've got a phone line sorted to the cabin now. That's the most important thing done. You need to stop baby-proofing everything. The Rayburn doesn't need to be fenced off, the furniture doesn't need to be wrapped in foam, and the bloody toilet seat doesn't need to have more security than Fort Knox.'

'Okay.'

'Is that an "okay, I'll put away the bubble wrap", or an "okay, let's placate the pregnant woman"?'

'I'll put baby-proofing on hold.'

'And sort the loo seat. I need to go again before we leave for the next scan.'

. . .

AN HOUR LATER, RORY STARED AT THE MOVING BLACK-AND-white image. This was what he needed to protect. His wife had not accidentally swallowed a basketball. A tiny defenceless human was inside her belly.

'Och, you're a wee wriggler.' The sonographer laughed.

'I think they're playing football,' said Zoe. 'That or break-dancing.'

Football's for plebs. Rugby's a real man's game. His father's words stole into the room like an icy draft. He gripped Zoe's hand tighter.

'Did you want to know the sex?' the sonographer asked.

Zoe glanced his way and raised her eyebrows as if checking he hadn't changed his mind from their last appointment.

He shook his head.

'No thanks,' she replied. 'We're going to keep it a surprise. Even though everyone thinks it's a boy, even me.'

Rory's heart thudded inside his chest. *Please, not a boy.* He rarely thought about his father. But ever since that second blue line had appeared on the pregnancy test, long-forgotten memories from his childhood awoke to slash at his heart and confidence.

'Well, not long to go now,' said the sonographer with a beaming smile. 'Next year you'll have your answer.'

Fear swelled inside him, squeezing each breath. He knew Zoe would be the best mum, but could he avoid being like his father? He tried to banish the thoughts with logic, but they still followed him whether he was awake or asleep, pushing all his buttons with laser-pointed accuracy. He didn't want to burden Zoe with his fears as she was exhausted and over-whelmed. Organising the perfect Christmas for the castle had stretched them to the limit and even though they'd brought in Duncan to help with running the estate, it still wasn't enough.

At least the festival of light was now underway. The

previous night the rain had held off and the gardens were packed as people wandered a trail through different light displays. Even though it was only late October, the local choir had sung carols, and everyone had been merry on mulled wine or hot chocolate.

'Can we stop and get a copy of *The Courier* before we head home?' Zoe asked as they left the hospital. 'I want to see the pictures from last night.'

He nodded. Thank god it had gone off without a hitch.

Ten minutes later he knew he shouldn't have counted his chickens.

'No!' cried Zoe. 'No, no, no, no!'

His fingers clenched around the steering wheel. 'What's wrong?'

'How did I miss this? Fuck! Rory, was this some kind of joke between you and Duncan?'

'What? What's a joke?'

She started crying.

Fuck! He scanned the road for a safe place to stop. 'Hang on.' He swerved into a layby, cut the engine and reached for her hand. 'What's happened?'

She passed him the paper.

The entirety of the front page was taken up with a report from the festival of light.

'Earl balls up at family event!' screamed the headline, and underneath, above the fold, was a photo of one of the displays. It was a small temple built by one of Rory's ancestors after returning from his Grand Tour in the seventeenth century. Circular, with thick stone columns that supported the roof – at the base of each column were a pair of large granite balls. Rory had never noticed the phallic nature of the structure. It was just another part of the castle. So he'd wrapped the columns and balls in fairy lights with Duncan, too busy meeting the deadline for either of them to look at their work with a critical eye. But now, illuminated in the darkness, it was obvious what it looked like.

Once again, the Earl of Kinloch seems determined to display the alleged dimensions of his personal endowments in public... This event is marketed at families, but with the amount of alcohol present and this lewd and immature display, people should think twice before attending... Another cheap publicity stunt by a man who supported the historically inaccurate and culturally offensive film Braveheart 2... "It's disgusting," an anonymous witness stated. "I had to explain to my grandson exactly why people were laughing so much."

He sighed.

The article didn't mention the wreath-making workshops, the carol singing, the kiddies nose-deep in hot chocolate with whipped cream and marshmallows. He'd been there from opening to closing and all he'd seen were happy faces. He didn't give two shits about the article, but he gave every shit about his wife's happiness and, right now, she was still crying.

'This is all my fault,' she hiccupped. 'I should have noticed. And now everything's ruined.'

He rubbed his thumb over the back of her hand. If this had happened when Zoe was less stressed and exhausted, she would have laughed it off, gleefully exclaiming about the extra publicity and putting a link to the article on the castle website. But now, she seemed devastated.

'It's not your fault,' he said. 'It's mine for not noticing. This article is bullshit. You saw how much everyone loved it. You've done something amazing.'

'It's a disaster. We need to take those lights down.'

'Fuck, no. Remember when you told me that all publicity is good publicity? I'm going to get Duncan to help me rig up more lights at the top of the columns. I want it to look like they're ejaculating onto the roof.'

Zoe snorted and his heart lifted.

'Maybe we can put a giant inflatable baby on the top?' he continued. 'Say it's an art installation celebrating your pregnancy?'

Her tears were turning into laughs. 'Don't you dare, Rory MacGinley.'

'And how about we start serving those "earl sausages" the butcher created last year? We can get the bakery to produce a "Zoe roll" to go with them.'

She shrieked with laughter and his heart soared. If he could make her smile everything would be okay.

NOVEMBER

32 weeks + four.

Third time lucky.

Zoe slowly typed 'Roryissexy' into the password box.

Access denied.

Feeling the first flickers of panic, she tried 'Roryissexy69', 'manbear69', and 'IlikebigScotsandIcannotlie'.

None of them worked.

She cradled her bump. *Breathe slowly in and out. Stress is bad for the baby. A crisis is an opportunity. Christmas is going to be perfect. You've got a month. A MONTH? FUCK!*

The castle website was their point of contact with the general public, and she was locked out.

'Everything okay, Zoe?' Duncan was looking at her with concern from across the estate office.

'I can't get into the website.'

'Can you reset the password?'

'No. I can't do anything. Have you been in the back end at all?'

He raised his hands in defence. 'No way. That's your domain. I just do whatever Rory tells me.'

She raised an eyebrow. 'You mean the jobs he doesn't want to do?'

He grinned. 'Fine by me. I'd rather be inside than out in all that.'

She glanced at the icy rain hurling itself at the windows. Winter was beginning to bite. Having Duncan working for them was a blessing and a curse. It helped with some of Rory's workload, but meant they hardly saw each other. Pregnancy hormones were making her hornier than ever, but a desk quickie was now impossible, and by the time they both returned to the cabin at night she was too exhausted. Her perfect Christmas was also not going according to plan. The bad weather meant lower numbers for the light festival, they were haemorrhaging money on electricity, and the friends of Brad who were hiring the castle over Christmas were more demanding than the love child of Madonna and Kim Jong-un. All ticket sales for the ceilidh were going through the website and now she couldn't get in.

'Do you think it's been hacked?' Duncan asked.

'God lord, no,' she bluffed. 'We're not the Pentagon. I'll ring customer support and see what's going on.'

Five minutes later, the enormity of the situation sank in. She'd missed updating the site plug-ins and a bot had gained access. As well as locking her out, all the financial details of anyone who'd bought a ticket to the ceilidh had been compromised. It was a fucking disaster.

DUNCAN WAS ON THE PHONE WORKING HIS WAY THROUGH the list of people who had purchased tickets when Rory arrived, his cheeks red from cold, his wet hair dripping onto the parquet floor.

'What can I do to help?' he asked.

'Dunc's ringing anyone who's bought a ticket and I'm on a live chat with a security company. We can't risk selling anything through the website so we're going to have to go old school. Posters up everywhere and tickets on the door or sold through the post office. Can I leave that job to you?'

He nodded. 'Date, time, location, price. Anything else?'

'Live band. And make sure they make the posters scream Christmas and party.'

He looked unsure. 'Any specific instructions? Do you want to see the design?'

She was trying to keep her focus on the online chat. There was no headspace left for another job.

'We don't have time. Just tell them to keep it simple. Red, holly, baubles. Anything that tells people it's a party and they're going to have fun.'

He nodded again and took out his phone.

HALF AN HOUR LATER THE WEBSITE WAS UNDER CONTROL and Zoe joined Duncan in contacting anyone whose details might have been compromised. In the background she could hear Rory fighting to keep his cool.

'It's a ceilidh. A party... Red, holly, balloons, the usual Christmas stuff... What? Yes, it's a party. A ceilidh... A party for ceilidh? What? The party *is* the ceilidh...' He ran his hands into his wet hair, grabbing clumps and tugging them away from his scalp. 'Look. Just keep it simple. Ceilidh, Christmas, Kinloch Castle. As long as people know where to come and when, and how much it costs, I don't care what the final design looks like.' He looked over at Zoe as if seeking her reassurance with this decision. She nodded. 'And we'll pay extra for you to put the posters up around Inverness and the villages around Kinloch,' he continued. 'You can send the tickets directly to Morag MacDougall at Kinloch post office.'

Zoe finished her call as Rory ended his. He opened his arms, and she was drawn into his warmth and security.

'Thank you,' she said into his chest.

'How can something that simple be so hard?' he grumbled. 'Did they not know what a ceilidh was?'

'They weren't Scottish, so I presume not. And it sounded like there was a TV in the background playing Formula One, so I think that's where their attention was.'

'We could always try another company?'

He shuddered. 'No way. One call like that is enough.' He hugged her tighter. 'Do you need anything else or can I go back to repairing a fence in the rain?'

'You'd rather do that than stay with me?' she teased.

'If Duncan wasn't here, I'd stay,' he whispered in her ear as he nuzzled her curly hair. 'You could always come with me?'

'I can't. There's too much to do.' She sighed. 'There's always too much to do.'

DECEMBER 1st
34 weeks

It didn't matter that there was a national mistletoe shortage. It didn't matter that the paying guests due in three weeks were impossible to please. It didn't matter that her bump was so big it was getting difficult to tie her boots. Zoe was so horny she couldn't think straight. Maybe it was the hormones, or perhaps orgasms were the best form of stress relief. But right now, she couldn't get enough, and her schedule hardly allowed for any.

She left Duncan in the estate office and waddled out of the castle to her truck, dialling Rory when she was inside.

'Everything okay?' he asked.

'Where are you?'

'The quarry. You alright?'

'I need you.'

'Can Duncan help? The charges are about to go off here.'

'I *need*, need you. So no, Duncan most definitely cannot help.'

'Ah.'

There was a pause. In the background she could hear the quarry siren, announcing the forthcoming explosion. She was sure Rory didn't really need to be there but knew how much he liked blowing things up.

'What about Bob?' he asked.

'Which one?'

'Fuck, I don't know. Bullet Bob?'

'Out of batteries.'

'Bunny Bob?'

'Basil found it and ate the ears off.'

'Oh. Bedtime Bob?'

'On charge and won't be ready for a few hours.'

'Back-up Bob?'

'Broke through overuse and is now Bandit's favourite chew toy.'

'Big Bob?'

'You're Big Bob.'

There was another pause. 'You heading back to the cabin?'

'Yes.'

'I'll be there in ten.'

BY THE TIME RORY ENTERED THE CABIN, ZOE WAS ON THE bed, extremely hot and bothered.

He toed off his boots. 'Let me give you a hand,' he said with a grin.

'Bloody big bump and bloody stupid socks!' she yelled.

He knelt in front of her and pulled them off, massaging her aching feet.

'You should be resting more.'

Zoe ignored him. She felt guilty enough for taking this time away from work. 'Oh my god that feels so good.'

Rory stroked up her calves, kneading the muscles. 'Would you like a massage and a nap?'

Her eyes snapped open. 'Rory MacGinley. I am so horny I could combust. The only massage I need right now is an internal one. Get naked. Now.'

He saluted her and tugged his shirt off.

Zoe swallowed as she watched the rippling muscles of his torso. She must have been Mother fucking Teresa in a former life to have been gifted Rory in this one. As his cock sprang free, she grabbed it greedily.

'Gimme, gimme.'

'I thought this was meant to be about you,' he said, his breath hitching as she stroked and squeezed him.

'I like Big Bob and I cannot lie,' she replied before sucking him deep.

'Zoe! Fuck!'

He tried to move but she held him firmly, her free hand tugging the weight of his balls. She loved giving him head. She loved the feel of him in her mouth, the way she could reduce this huge strong man to a shaking mess.

'Zoe, seriously, it's been too long, I'm—'

She released him with a pop.

He gritted his teeth, the tendons in his neck strained. His breath rushed out with a whoosh as he regained control. His arctic blue eyes fixed her with a stare that could melt diamonds.

He pointed to the headboard. 'Get up there and hold on tight.'

Her thighs clenched and she scooted back, kneeling up and facing away from him. She moaned as his hand cupped her from behind, running his fingers through the slickness of her arousal. The pregnancy made everything feel fuller, more sensitive. He bit her neck and thrust two fingers inside.

'Yes!' she cried, arching into his touch.

She was already so close. She could feel the hardness of his shaft as she rocked back against him. He held her breast with his other hand, pinching and tugging her nipple. She gasped as sensation sparked, sending shocks of light through her. His thumb found her clit and she bucked frantically into his hand. He growled into her neck and the vibrations sent her over the edge, her muscles convulsing as her orgasm hit. Rory held her tightly, continuing to nip, pinch and rub every point of pleasure as she fell apart in his arms.

As her breath slowed, he pulled his fingers from her.

'Rory,' she whined.

He pressed his cock between her thighs and she squeezed around it.

'Is this what you want?' he asked, his voice gravelly and deep.

'Yes, yes, yes!' One orgasm had barely scratched the surface of her need.

He moved the thick length back and forwards, coating it in her juices.

'And how do you want it, Zoe?'

His body covered hers, his hands roaming over her breasts, her belly.

'Hard,' she gasped.

He nudged her knees wider, and she angled her bottom up. The feel of the fat head of his shaft nudging into her was the most exquisite relief. He moved slowly as she adjusted to his size, brushing his fingers over her clit and sending more urgent rushes of pleasure through her to pop and fizz across her skin.

'More, Rory. I need more.'

He pushed deeper and she wriggled back against him until

he filled her completely. She sighed with pleasure. Her body, mind and soul were full of him and she could never get enough.

He withdrew slowly, then pushed forward. His pace was slow and steady, building the fire inside her.

'Faster, Rory. Harder.'

She gripped the headboard and met his thrusts with her own, but he was still holding back.

'Wait,' he growled.

He held her hip steady with one hand, the other teasing her clitoris. 'One more orgasm won't be enough,' he stated.

She whimpered.

'Touch your breasts. I've got you.'

She released her hands from the end of the bed and tugged her nipples. He rolled her clit between his fingers and thumb.

'Oh my god, oh my god,' she moaned.

His cock continued to move. In, out. In, out. The pressure was rising. In, out, in, out. Pleasure bubbled and boiled inside her. Her breaths came faster as he rocked her higher.

'Yes, yes, yes.'

He pinched her clitoris and she detonated with a scream. He thrusted faster, chasing her orgasm over the cliff as she cried out, again and again.

The sensations rolled on and on. He thrust harder, pounding into her as he strummed her clitoris.

'Rory! I'm going to come again,' she wailed.

He pulled her body closer, angling her head so he could kiss her, his hips snapping faster. Another climax barrelled through, stealing her breath and filling her head with stars. He wrenched his head from hers as he lost control, crying her name, his hips jerking as he came inside her.

'Zoe, Zoe, Zoe.'

She slumped forward and he eased her down to the bed, cradling her as she lay on her side.

'I love you so much,' she mumbled.

'I love you too,' he murmured, nuzzling into her hair.

He held her close as she drifted off to sleep.

❧

RORY SANDED THE PIECE OF WOOD UNTIL IT WAS AS SMOOTH as silk. He'd left Zoe to rest and returned to his workshop to finish the crib he was making for their baby. It had various iterations and was able to fit flush with the edge of the bed, as well as expand to stand on its own. He'd declined the offer of a suite of nursery furniture from his mother and Brad. He didn't want anything he hadn't made, and he was sure the baby didn't need more furniture than the entire east wing of the castle.

They wanted to live in the cabin for as long as possible after the baby was born. However, he knew someday they would have to leave it behind and make the castle their permanent home. The imposing building still held echoes of his father. The thump of his boots, the bark of his voice, the crack of his whip against the stonework. The only way Rory could think to avoid being him was to make sure everything he did was the polar opposite to his brutish behaviour. But no matter how he tried to reassure himself with logic, fear still crept in.

His phone pinged with a message.

TABI: What's up?

He sighed and shook his head. Was this woman a witch?

RORY: Don't ever go to Salem. They'll burn you.

TABI: Ha! Knew it, Bagpipes. Tell Auntie Tabi what's got your kilt in a twist.

RORY: The whole parent thing. Are you worried about being like your dad? Making the same mistakes?

TABI: I don't have the same issues. I hope I'm more like him and less like me. He's stubborn but he's a good dad. A bit of a worrier, but

I'm kind of off the rails sometimes. Trust me, all parents make mistakes and you're not going to be like yours. It's our job to fuck our kids up in a whole new way.

RORY: How can you be so sure you'll do it differently?

TABI: Because I'm self-aware enough to stop repeating the same patterns, and I've got Bax. And anyway, we've got a whole nature vs nurture thing going if we even get to adopt kids since they won't be from my junk.

TABI: You're really worried you'll be like your parents?

RORY: Sometimes, yes.

TABI: Zoe's parents are cool, right? They tolerate you?

RORY: Yeah, they're lovely.

TABI: Do Zoe's friends like you?

RORY: They seem to.

TABI: Do you think Zoe would have married you if you were like your dad?

RORY: No fucking way.

TABI: And do you think Zoe would let you behave like your dad?

RORY: Okay, okay, I get it.

TABI: I'm always right. Just ask Bax.

RORY: Thanks. I just can't believe I'm going to have a kid. It's the scariest thing I've ever done.

TABI: You've got this. If you can cope with Brad Bauer as a stepfather, then you can cope with anything. He's kind of ridic.

RORY: NOT MY STEPFATHER!

TABI: Lol. You're so easy to wind up.

TABI: Christmas with Bauer's friends still happening?

RORY: Yes. We've got a couple of weeks to turn the castle into the bloody Downton Abbey *Christmas special and it's not going well.*

TABI: Not enough sheep intestines or blood pudding to go around?

RORY: Mistletoe shortage and we underestimated how long it would take to decorate the castle the way they want it.

TABI: Well at least you've got the Christmas lights sorted. Those massive schlongs in the garden look real fancy. Want some wine to impress them?

RORY: Sigh. Yes. Send loads. If they're drunk, perhaps they'll think it's perfect.

DECEMBER 10TH

35 weeks + 2

DUNCAN: There's only one cracker left in the box.

RORY: On my way.

Entering the back door of the castle at a run, Rory leapt up the stairs. This latest message from Duncan told him things were extremely suboptimal in his wife's world. He could hear the anguish in her voice carrying down the corridor as he strode towards the estate office door. God only knew how she'd react when she saw what was in his jacket pocket.

'How are they meant to have chestnuts roasting on an open fire when the chestnuts are already cooked, peeled and vacu-packed?' she yelled into the phone as he entered the room.

Rory nodded at Duncan who beat a hasty retreat. On the floor were cardboard boxes filled with provisions they'd ordered for Brad's friends who were arriving in just over a week.

'And I ordered mince pies, not mince beef pies,' she continued. There was a pause. 'No! Mince pies as in the dried fruity things. You've sent sodding Fray Bentos ones with actual mince in them. And a bog-standard fruit cake is not, I repeat, not, an acceptable substitute for Christmas cake!'

She was close to tears. He took her hand and gave it a squeeze.

'You don't seem to understand how important this is,' she said, her voice wavering. 'How important Christmas is. It's going to be ruined.' Her chin started to wobble. 'I'll call you back.'

She hung up and sobbed into his chest.

'It's a complete disaster,' she cried. 'I can't seem to get anything right.'

'It's not your fault. We can order pies and cakes from Margaret at the bakery.'

'We can't. They wanted ones that came wrapped in cellophane and had some poncey label on. Honestly, Rory, I can't please them.' She raised her head. 'What are you doing back?'

He took a deep breath. It would be better if she found out in private.

'It's not the end of the world, but—'

'Oh my god, what's happened?'

'Shhhh, it's okay.' He pulled a folded poster from his jacket pocket. 'This one's on me. I'm sorry. The printers well and truly cocked it up.'

Zoe opened it out. He'd spotted it stapled to a telegraph pole – a poster advertising the Christmas ceilidh.

'A Christmas *Kayleigh*?' Zoe screamed.

The location, date and time were all correct, but the poster looked like it was advertising a little girl's birthday party. The baubles they'd discussed looked like balloons, and the background was more bubble gum pink than Santa red.

'I'm sorry, Zoe, it's my fault. They didn't seem to know what a ceilidh was and I didn't spell it for them.'

'Do the tickets say the same thing?' she asked faintly.

He nodded. 'I went to the post office. They've just been delivered and they all say Christmas Kayleigh.'

She sank her head. '*The Courier* is going to have a fucking field day with this one. They're going to blame me because I'm English.'

His hands formed into fists. 'I'll tell them it was me.'

She sighed. 'They won't care. I don't think there's any way we can spin this.'

Rory pulled out his phone and rang Clive, the owner of Kinloch's only pub who was supplying the bar for the ceilidh. He put it on speaker so Zoe could listen in.

'Clive, it's Rory and Zoe here. When's your Kayleigh's birthday?'

'Next month. It's her 21st. Why?'

'Have you seen the posters for the ceilidh yet?'

'No.'

'The printers fucked up big time and it looks like we're throwing a party for her.'

'You're joking?'

'No.'

Clive laughed. 'God, she'll either be mortified or think it's the best thing ever.'

'I want to try and turn this around,' continued Rory. 'Could you speak to Kayleigh and ask if she wants to invite her friends? We can give her fifty free tickets if she's happy to turn this into an early birthday party?'

'Will do. I'll speak to her now and ring you back.'

'Thanks, Clive.'

Rory ended the call.

'Thank you.' Zoe smiled. 'That's a brilliant idea.'

He shrugged. 'First time for everything.'

'Nonsense. You're amazing. It's me who's falling apart.'

He pulled her into his arms. 'You're eight months pregnant and haven't taken a proper day off in months. You're doing great.'

'Did you get the tree for the entrance hall?'

'Yeah, want to go and see it?'

OH GOD. JUST NO.

Zoe bit the inside of her cheek to stop the scream of frustration escaping. She couldn't piss all over her husband's handiwork. Rory may have chopped down a tree taller than any cottage in Kinloch, but in the entrance hall of the castle it looked embarrassingly small. She'd already vastly underestimated the volume of decorations needed to turn the castle into a Hallmark Christmas special, and now they were also dealing with a national shortage of mistletoe and holly. Brad's friends were expecting a winter wonderland, but instead were going to get one from Poundland. The worst thing was that Rory had decorated the tree with every bauble they had, and it still looked completely under-dressed.

He had a worried frown on his face. 'Is it okay? It's the first tree I've ever decorated.'

Don't cry, don't cry, don't cry.

She burst into tears.

'Zoe, love, what's wrong? Just tell me and I'll fix it.'

'It's too small and you've gone to so much effort and I'm a terrible person and I can't cope and I'm losing my mind,' she wailed.

He ran his hands into his hair. 'I'll sort it. I'll find a way.'

'There isn't a way, Rory. We've run out time, and I'm the one to blame. I wanted the extra ceilidh, the festival of lights, the sodding Santa experience. I said yes to Brad's friends. Christmas is ruined and it's all my fault.'

DECEMBER 18th
36 weeks + 3

Zoe looked at her reflection in the mirror and tried not to cry. Again. It was the day Santa was visiting Kinloch Castle and she was in a room just off the entrance hall, trying to fit her heavily pregnant body into an elf costume. This had seemed a brilliant idea eight months ago, but even an extra-large costume wasn't going to cut it. The striped tights only made it as far as her mid-thigh and the top was stuck above her bump. She looked like an overstuffed sausage and felt like a beached whale. This was her favourite time of the year, and she was finally going to be a mum. She should have been full of happiness. However, right now, she hated being pregnant and hated Christmas. Her stomach seemed unnaturally big, her ankles were swollen, she couldn't sleep, she needed to pee all the time and her breasts had started leaking.

She felt guilty and ungrateful and desperately missed her

best friend, Sam, and her parents. Her mum and dad had planned to stay home for Christmas, then travel up after Zoe gave birth in January and stay a month. But even if they changed their plans, there was nowhere for them to stay. Brad's friends were due in a couple of days and had hired the entire castle. This Christmas was meant to be quiet, just her and Rory together in the cabin, but was now looking like more relentless work when she could barely stay on her feet.

She took off the elf costume and put her maternity trousers back on. They were down an elf but at least Rory was still playing Father Christmas. There was a knock at the door, and he entered, a big smile on his face.

'I bring glad tidings.'

She looked at him askance. 'Have you been on the sherry?'

'Of great joy,' he continued.

Her jaw dropped. He looked relieved as well as happy. This was extremely strange. 'Who are you and what have you done with my husband?' she demanded.

He cradled her face and brushed his lips across hers. 'I have done a good thing.'

'And that thing is?'

'Brad's friends aren't coming.'

She pulled back. 'What? They cancelled? But we need the money! We've spent—'

'Shhhh, it's okay. We're not refunding them anything.'

'What? How?'

'I rang Brad. I told him about the stress we're under, the mistletoe shortage and how we didn't want his friends to be disappointed.'

'You rang Brad?'

He nodded.

'He Who Shall Not Be Named?'

He grinned. 'Yup. And he persuaded them to swap coming

83

here for a free stay at his place in Aspen followed by Saint Barts.'

'And we don't have to give them their money back?'

'Nope.'

She sank into a chair, holding his hand. 'Holy shit. So we can have a quiet Christmas, just the two of us?'

'Yes, or if you want, we can invite your parents?'

She welled up. 'Thank you, Rory. This is such a relief. I can't believe it.'

'Now all we need to do is get today over with, then you can put your feet up. You, me, Bandit, Basil and your beautiful bump. I promise I'll make Christmas perfect for you.'

She swallowed her emotion down. 'Okay, let's get you dressed as Santa and put some talc in your beard to make it white.'

Zoe had deliberately ordered an XXL Santa suit. He took off his work trousers and pulled on the red velour bottoms.

Oh god.

Being six foot six, they only reached his knees. It looked like he was wearing lederhosen. Neither of them said a word. He put the top on. It was big enough around the middle, but the sleeves ended just below his elbows. It was another Christmas clusterfuck.

The ring of Rory's phone filled the silence.

'It's Brad.' He took the call.

'Dude!' Brad was so loud it sounded like he was in the room with them. 'Where are you, man?'

'We're in the castle.'

'Where?'

'Um, in the small study off the entrance hall. Why?'

The door flew open and Brad bounded in. 'Surprise!'

Zoe gripped Rory's hand as they stared at him in silence. Barbara entered after Brad and looked Rory up and down.

'Oh dear. That really won't do. Think of the children. You'll terrify them.'

Rory managed to recover first. 'Mum,' he croaked. 'What are you doing here?'

'Isn't it obvious? We're putting family first. You made it clear how much the two of you were struggling, and Zoe needs to rest.'

'But what about Fight Dragon Club?' Zoe asked. 'Isn't that meant to be filming now?'

Brad clicked his fingers. 'Rescheduled. I didn't want to miss the birth of my grandson.'

'I'm not due till mid-January,' Zoe said, feeling light-headed.

'Jesus says it's his time.'

'Jesús, Bradley. How many times do we have to have this conversation?'

'Sorry, Countess.'

Barbara raised her eyes theatrically, then clicked her fingers at Rory. 'Give Bradley the costume. We can take it from here.'

ZOE STOOD BEHIND BRAD IN THE CASTLE LIBRARY, NEXT TO the huge open fire, a clipboard in her hands, and watched him distil Christmas into the spirit of pure commercialism.

It hadn't started well.

She'd put a chair out for the children to sit on, but the first boy, who was clearly a fan, stood to attention in front of Brad.

'I want an Xbox,' he said loudly.

His mother stood behind her son, shaking her head at Brad.

'A bike,' she stage-whispered. 'He wants a bike.'

'Ho, ho, ho,' overacted Brad. 'I think what you *really* want is a *bike*.'

The little boy shook his head so hard Zoe was worried it might fly off.

'No! I want an Xbox.' There was a pause. 'Please?'

Brad slapped his thigh. 'Well, with manners like that, how can I refuse! One Xbox coming your way!'

The boy fist-pumped. 'Yessssss!'

His mother looked miserable.

Zoe dashed forward. 'You can't promise that,' she whispered in Brad's ear. 'She can't afford it.'

'Just take her details, babe. Father Bradmas has got this.'

It went downhill from there.

Within half an hour of him posting a photo of himself dressed as Santa, queues formed out of the castle for the chance to sit on his knee. And when word got out that he would provide whatever you asked for, the demands escalated.

'Are you sure you want a Tesla?' Brad asked a little girl who really should have been asking for two front teeth.

'Yeth,' she replied. 'A Tethla. And it hath to be...' she broke off to look at her father.

'Deep blue metallic,' he said out of the corner of his mouth.

'Theep boo methallic,' she repeated.

NINETY MINUTES IN, RORY SHUT THE MAIN DOORS.

Ninety-one minutes in, fights broke out and people started smashing windows. Shortly after, the riot police arrived, along with two ambulances and the local press.

Barbara, toting a loaded shotgun, escorted Zoe out the back door, took her back to the cabin, then returned to the castle.

Zoe got into bed, cuddling Basil.

Merry Fucking Christmas.

. . .

DECEMBER 21ST
36 weeks + 6

It was official. Zoe was done with being pregnant and done with Christmas. She'd spent so long making the holiday magical for other people there was no magic left for her. She was heavy and depressed, and nothing could lift her mood. Rory was busy working outside, but she didn't even have the energy to ask about his days. She just stayed at the cabin with Bandit and Basil, hiding from everyone and counting the days till her parents arrived.

That morning she'd woken with a dodgy stomach and by the time Rory arrived back, late afternoon, she was ready for bed.

'Get dressed,' he said. 'We're going into town.'

'Don't want to,' she grumbled. 'I'm fed up and my tummy's upset. That steak you fed me last night didn't agree with me.'

He frowned. 'I ate most of it and I'm okay. You don't think it's anything to do with the baby?'

She shrugged. 'Who knows? Pregnancy sucks and I could have another six weeks of it.'

'Well, there's a special carol service in Kinloch this evening and I really want to go.'

'Carols? You?'

'I think your love of Christmas has rubbed off on me.'

'I'm not in love anymore. It's all a load of consumerist bollocks. You were right. It's just another made-up holiday to be endured.'

He ran his hand through his hair. 'Zoe, I'm sorry I couldn't do more to take the strain off you. But I do want you to remember why you love Christmas.'

'And a carol concert will do that?'

'You never know. There's going to be candles. And mince pies.'

She rolled her eyes.

'Please? For me?'

She threw up her arms. 'Okay, okay. I'll do it. Can I get away with putting a coat over my pyjamas?'

He hesitated. 'If you don't mind the village seeing them?'

'I don't care right now. I've been trying for perfection, but everything's gone tits up no matter what I do.'

She threw on her coat, hat and boots and followed Rory out to his truck, Bandit following. He'd been especially attentive recently and now wouldn't leave her side. Rory drove into the back courtyard and led her through the castle into the great hall. It was already full of people, and everyone was holding a candle. With the main lights turned low, Zoe had to admit it was a beautiful sight. Rory led her to the front where one of the castle's wooden thrones had been placed.

'Are you sure I can sit?' she whispered. 'Everyone else is standing.'

'It's your castle, and no one else is eight and a half months pregnant,' he whispered back.

She sank gratefully into the chair as the Kinloch community choir filed onto the raised dais at one end of the hall and began to sing.

'The angel Gabriel from heaven came,
his wings as drifted snow, his eyes as flame;
"All hail," said he, "thou lowly maiden Mary,
most highly favoured lady." Gloria.'

Zoe held her breath as the music filled the space. In the half-light she could imagine this scene taking place hundreds, if not thousands, of years ago.

The carol ended and Brad's voice rang out. 'And in the sixth month, the angel Gabrielle was sent from God into a city of Galilee, called Nazareth.'

The choir parted and a figure stepped forward, dressed all in white, with fairy wings and a tinsel halo.

Zoe's mouth fell open. *Sam?* But wasn't she meant to be working abroad?

Sam raised a magic wand in Zoe's direction and a spotlight suddenly shone on her chair.

What the fuck?

'Hail Mary, full of grace,' Sam declaimed. 'The Lord is with thee! Blessed art thou amongst women.'

Zoe turned to look at Rory, but he'd disappeared.

'Fear not, Mary,' Sam continued. 'For your husband shall returneth sooneth. He might have just poppeth out for a quick bathroom breaketh.' Laughter rippled around the room. 'Behold! Thou shalt conceive in thy womb, and bring forth a son or daughter, and thou shalt name him or her whatever the hell you chooseth.'

'Babe! Stick to the script!' Brad hissed from the side.

'The child shall be great, and the Lord God shall give unto him the throne of Rory his father; and he shall reign in the house of Kinloch forever.'

The audience applauded loudly.

'And Mary said unto the angel,' said Brad, looking pointedly at Zoe.

'Er,' Zoe began, trying to rack her brains for the next line. 'Um, but how has this happeneth? For I know not a man.'

'The Holy Ghost shall come upon thee,' said Sam. 'But in a totally consensual, non-creepy manner, so don't freaketh out.'

'And Mary said,' continued Brad.

Fuck! What *did* Mary say? 'Um, thanks for that,' Zoe replied. 'Now you're here, anything else I should know?'

'Not at all,' replied Brad, quickly. 'Then the angel departed from her.' He gestured for Sam to move but she didn't budge. 'Forthwith, and at great speed!' he continued.

'But the angel Gabrielle had just remembered a few more things to sayeth,' Sam continued. 'Like how Mary is a hot milf, and she can totes see her and Gabrielle becoming BFF-eths.'

Brad stepped onto the dais in front of Sam, his hands raised to stop the laughter.

'And lo! There appeareth Joseph, who was most pleased because the Holy Ghost had come to him in a dream and explained the situation, so he was totally cool about everything.'

Rory returned to her side wearing a rag rug held up by a belt over his clothes and a tea towel on his head.

'What's going on?' she whispered.

'You only got to play the giraffe in your school's nativity, so I thought you deserved a crack at the main role.'

He took another tea towel, placed it on her head and secured it with a woven circlet.

Her heart was so full she didn't know whether to laugh or cry.

'So, what happens next?' she asked.

'And it came to pass that a decree went out from Caesar Augustus that all the world should be registered,' said Brad. 'Joseph went up from Galilee to Bethlehem, to be registered with Mary, his betrothed wife, who was heavy with child.'

Rory held out his hand and Zoe stood. The choir started singing 'Little Donkey' as they processed out of the hall. Everyone followed them.

'Am I going to have to get on the back of a donkey?' she hissed.

He grinned. 'Just wait and see.'

❧ 9 ❧

Z oe exited the castle through the main entrance and started laughing. In front of her was an old open-topped carriage, and pulling it were two Highland cows. A sign stuck to the side read: 'DONKEY'.

One of the cows mooed loudly.

'Is that Zoe?' she asked excitedly.

Rory nodded. 'She was desperate to play the front half of the donkey.'

There was a loud noise as the other cow dumped a large pat on the cobbles.

'And that one's playing the back end,' he continued with a grin.

He helped her into the carriage and Bandit jumped in after.

'You're not sitting here with me?'

Rory shook his head. 'I'm going to lead them. And anyway, I wasn't sure how much weight they could pull.'

Brad had commandeered himself a megaphone and continued the story.

'And so, Mary and Joseph began their journey to Bethlehem,' he yelled. 'Picture the scene. Travelling alone through the desert: one pregnant virgin, one humble carpenter, and one donkey. The fate of the world resting in Mary's untouched womb.'

The cows set off at a slow pace through the courtyard, followed by the rest of the village with their candles. The choir were up ahead, on their umpteenth rendition of 'Little Donkey'.

A sharp pain sliced across Zoe's stomach. She gasped, clutching the side of the carriage. It got stronger, stopping her breath as it tightened around her stomach. Just as she thought she might pass out, it stopped.

What the ever-loving fuck was that?

There was no way this was labour. She wasn't due for another three weeks and knew most first-time mums gave birth ten days after their estimated date. Could it be Braxton Hicks contractions? She looked around. People were smiling and chatting. Rory's attention was ahead with the cows. No one was looking at her.

Okay, breathe. Nothing to worry about. Chill the fuck out.

It slammed back into her, squeezing her body till there was nothing left but blinding pain. This time she remembered to breathe. She closed her eyes, forcing the air in and out. When it finally stopped, she was trembling. Bandit whined and nudged up against her.

'It's okay, buddy. I'm fine.'

She clenched her jaw to fight back tears. If this was indeed early labour, she wasn't going to survive. Wasn't it meant to be like period pain? Pop a couple of paracetamol, have a hot bath and go to bed? If she'd just had two mild contractions, then fuck only knew what major ones felt like. And she couldn't stop the nativity for a false alarm.

The procession paused at the bottom of the high street by

a small area of grass where the war memorial stood. On it, behind a barrier, were three men trying to control a small flock of badly behaved sheep. She saw Duncan, Fiona's younger brother, Jamie, and—

Zoe blinked.

'Dad?'

Her father looked up and gave a wave. 'Hi, love!' The sheep nearest him grabbed a mouthful of his robe and pulled. There was a loud rip and suddenly he was showing the village his boxer shorts and knobbly knees.

'Behold,' yelled Duncan over the baaing of the sheep. 'I am sore afraid!

'Aye,' continued Jamie. 'Me too. Is that an angel?'

'Sure is, babe,' replied Sam, giving him a wink.

'I bring you good news of great joy,' yelled Brad into his megaphone.

'Oy!' Sam yelled back. 'That's my line! For there is born to you this day—'

Zoe was hit by another wall of pain. She clutched Bandit's fur and tried to breathe through it.

'Fuck, fuck, fuck, fuck,' she muttered.

'A saviour who is Christ the lord or lady, and you will find him or her wrapped in bandages like a freaking mummy or something—'

'In a manger!' screamed Brad.

'I was just getting to that bit!'

The choir started singing 'While Shepherds Watched Their Flocks' as the sheep alternated between baaing and emptying their bowels. The noise was loud enough to drown out Zoe's frantic swearing.

Rory pulled the cows past the shepherds as her dad called out to her, 'See you in a bit, love!'

She managed to wave before being hit with another freight

train of a contraction. What had Fiona told her? Labour usually went on for days and wasn't serious unless she couldn't talk? At the moment she could still formulate a sentence, however, every word appeared to be 'fuck'. As the pain passed, she caught her breath. Rory turned.

'You enjoying yourself?' he asked with a smile.

She gave him two thumbs up and managed a manic grin. He looked so happy. She wasn't going to ruin his surprise by making a fuss about nothing.

The choir continued singing as they proceeded down the high street towards the post office. Outside, dressed as if they'd been attacked by velour curtains from the seventies, stood Zoe's mum, Fiona, and Fiona's mum, Morag. The choir segued into 'We Three Kings'.

When the carol finished, Morag spoke. 'We are three wise women who have been following a star.'

Brad leapt in front of them, wearing glow bands around his neck, head and wrists, looking like an over-medicated raver who'd crashed into a school disco.

'That's me, baby! I'm the star!'

The crowd whooped and clapped, their attention thankfully away from Zoe as she braced against the carriage, moaning in pain.

'We bring gifts of gold,' said Zoe's mum.

'Frankenstein,' added Morag.

'And Prosecco and spiced shortbread!' finished Fiona.

Everyone cheered.

As another contraction smacked into her, she caught Sam's eye.

Her friend frowned and mouthed, 'you okay?'

Zoe nodded, her nails digging into her thigh. It was all getting too much. She'd never experienced pain like this before. It was so intense and all-consuming she wanted to throw up. She needed to get through this nativity, then get to Raigmore hospital. She didn't care if she was days or even weeks away from giving birth. She needed pain relief right now. That, or sudden death.

She ran the nativity story through her head. Hopefully they would skip Herod and the massacre of the innocents. What was still left? Brad was now telling everyone how Mary and Joseph had survived the journey to Bethlehem and were trying to find somewhere to stay. The procession stopped outside The King's Arms and Rory knocked on the door.

Clive opened it.

'Kind sir,' Rory started. 'My wife is heavy with child and we need a place to stay.'

'There's no room at the inn,' said Clive.

A contraction slammed into Zoe and she screamed with pain.

'See?' declaimed Rory, dramatically. 'The baby draws near.'

'Sorry, mate. No can do,' Clive replied, crossing his arms in front of his chest.

The crowd booed and Bandit barked. Zoe was now panting to stay conscious.

'Not even a lowly stable?' asked Rory.

Clive sighed theatrically. 'Well, I suppose you could use it as long as you stay out of the way of the oxen. It's back down yonder high street in the community centre.'

'Thank you,' replied Rory. 'We shall travel there forthwith.'

He turned the cows in a slow circle and they started back down the road. Zoe closed her eyes. She couldn't take anything else in. She was vaguely aware of singing and laughing, and Bandit licking her hand, but most of her concentration was taken up in preparing for the battering waves of agony that relentlessly assaulted her. She was lost in a turbulent sea of pain that crashed through without mercy.

'Behold!' yelled Brad into his megaphone.

Zoe opened her eyes. In front of them, at the end of a small car park, was the entrance to the community centre. A large sign above the door read 'LOWLY STABLE' and a beautifully decorated Christmas tree stood to the side. The crowds fell silent as the choir sang 'Oh Tannenbaum'.

Another contraction slammed into her, and she screamed.

'Zoe?' Rory dropped the halter holding the cows and rushed to the side of the carriage. 'What's wrong?'

She panted, unable to get any words out, her eyes scrunched closed.

The carriage jolted forwards.

Bandit barked loudly.

She opened her eyes to see the cows heading straight for the tree.

Rory leapt up next to her. 'What's happening? Is it the baby?'

There was a crash and the carriage stopped with a jolt. The cows had knocked the tree over and were investigating the decorations.

'Let's get you inside.' Rory lifted her out and carried her into the building.

She could hear Bandit snarling and growling at the door, preventing anyone from following them.

The community centre was small and had only one main room, which had been decorated to look like a stable, with loose straw and bales all over the floor.

Rory placed her gently onto a bale and she fell forward onto her hands and knees, circling her hips and lowing like a cow.

'Is this labour?'

She nodded, her whole body undulating with pain.

'Fuck! Hang on. I'll go get help.'

Her hand shot out to grip his wrist. 'Don't. Leave. Me,' she panted.

'But—'

She dug her nails into his arm.

'Okay. I won't leave. I promise. What can I do?'

'Need. Pyjamas. Off,' she managed.

'Someone call an ambulance!' Rory yelled. 'I think she's having the baby!'

She clung to him as he held her up and tugged off her pyjama bottoms. Her body had completely taken over and all she could do was hang on for dear life. The pain was moving down in waves, then she had a sudden, overwhelming urge to push. She could just about make out people yelling her name and Bandit barking and growling. Rory pulled off her coat.

'I've got you, Zoe. I'm here.'

She was on her knees, facing him. He held under her shoulders, kissing the side of her head and reassuring her.

'I love you. You've got this. It's okay.'

A stinging circle of pain stretched her as another massive contraction pushed down. There was no going back. It was happening and there was nothing she could do to stop it.

'Rory!' she screamed as she felt her baby's head pop out. There was a lull, and she caught her breath.

She stared into Rory's worried eyes. 'The head's out,' she panted. 'You need to be ready to catch them.'

His face was pale, but he nodded. 'Just let me know when.'

Another contraction rolled through. 'Now!'

She held around his neck as his hands moved between her legs.

The baby slipped out.

'I've got them,' he said. 'I've got them.'

She fumbled to open her top and he lifted the baby to rest on her chest, cradling the two of them in his massive arms.

They looked down at their child. It had a shock of ginger hair and deep dark eyes that stared up at them solemnly.

'Oh my god,' she gasped, her body filled with a rush of overwhelming love. 'We did it.'

They held each other, their baby between them as they cried and laughed.

'You're incredible,' Rory whispered.

'Me or the baby?'

'You, hands down. But this little one is pretty incredible too.'

'What's going on in there?' Barbara yelled from the front door. 'Bandit won't let anyone in!'

The baby let out a loud cry.

'It's a boy!' screamed Brad.

Rory shook his head as the choir launched into 'Joy to the World'.

Zoe angled the baby towards her breast and it immediately latched on.

'Shall we see what we've got?' she asked.

Rory nodded and carefully moved the umbilical cord to one side. 'I think it's a girl,' he said, sounding dazed.

'Are you sure?'

He lifted one leg up. 'Yes. I can confirm there is no penis to be found.'

Zoe kissed her daughter's head. 'Thank you for proving everyone wrong,' she whispered.

❧

RORY: (PICTURE OF BABY)
  TABI: OMG is that yours?
  SABRINA: Wait, what? Has Zoe had it?
  JONATHAN: Oh my goodness, congratulations, my friend!

SABRINA: But she's due next year!

RORY: The baby came early.

TRISTAN: Congratulations!

SABRINA: OMG OMG OMG! What did you have?

TABI: Just checked Brad's feed. You had a boy?

BEN: Congratulations, Rory! How's Zoe doing?

RORY: She's doing great considering everything.

TABI: Did he come out via the sunroof?

SABRINA: What's his name????

RORY: Zoe had a precipitous labour. It lasted less than an hour.

TRISTAN: Fucking hell that sounds intense.

RORY: She went into labour in a carriage pulled by two Highland cows during a retelling of the nativity.

TABI: What. The. Fuck???

SABRINA: No frikking way!!!

BEN: Did she give birth in a stable?

RORY: Almost. The community centre. On a bed of straw. I was the only person there as Bandit wouldn't let anyone else in.

TABI: Have you called him Jesus?

RORY: We've named her Shona.

SABRINA: Her???

RORY: Yeah. I love it when my mother's husband gets it wrong.

RORY: (Multiple photos of Shona)

SABRINA: Awwwwwwwwwwwwww!!!!!!

BEN: I see she's got her mother's hair.

RORY: I know. She's so beautiful I can't stop staring at her.

TABI: You big Scottish softie.

RORY: Don't care. I've never been happier.

SABRINA: I'm crying!!!!!!!

BEN: Just showed Laurie. Now she's crying.

TRISTAN: Sherilyn too.

JONATHAN: So much emotion! Can't wait to show Juliet!

RORY: Gotta go. I'll send more photos later. I think I've turned into one of those dads I swore blind I'd never be...

TABI: Fatherhood suits you, Bagpipes. Give Shona and Zoe a kiss from all of us.

RORY: Will do.

EPILOGUE

CHRISTMAS DAY

R ory padded quietly around the inside of the cabin, Shona cradled against his bare chest. Even though she seemed to have a talent for sleeping that rivalled her mother's, he couldn't help the one-sided conversation that flowed from him like a river into the loch.

'So, even though your mummy is currently sparko, when she wakes up, it's very important to have a cup of tea ready. Especially now she's also responsible for feeding you, little one,' he whispered. 'Although the kettle boiling might be too noisy. Maybe we should go for a walk with Bandit?'

Shona stirred, her tiny lips smacking together. Rory's heart felt too full for his chest, love overflowing and turning his insides to mush.

He kissed her forehead. 'I love you, Shona.'

A groan came from the bed as Zoe opened her eyes. 'What time is it?' she mumbled.

'Nearly half ten. We're due at the castle at twelve. Happy Christmas.'

'We can't have sex for the next six weeks.'

'Err. I wasn't trying to?'

'Well, the sight of you shirtless and holding a baby is inspiring me to make more, so try and make yourself a little less attractive.'

He smiled. 'I haven't brushed my hair.'

'You never brush it.'

He sat on the edge of the bed and handed Shona to Zoe for the morning feed.

'I can't believe she's here,' she said quietly. 'We're so lucky.'

Rory squeezed her hand. He'd never been one for displays of emotion, but he seemed to be on an oxytocin high that was never going down.

'It's snowing,' he said.

She looked worried. 'Will we be able to get to the castle?'

'Yes, it's only light but it looks really pretty. You'll love it.'

She smiled. 'This is the best Christmas ever.'

'So far. Don't forget we've got to survive lunch.'

'Do you know who's in charge?'

He raised an eyebrow. 'Who do you think? Mum and Brad are incapable of relinquishing control over anything. Thank god your folks are so easy-going.'

'There'll be others to help too.'

'Yes, it should be fun.'

She looked at him as if he'd just grown another head. 'Fun? You're looking forward to Christmas Day?'

He smiled. 'Your obsession has rubbed off on me. I'm a changed man.'

She ran her fingers down his jaw. 'Well, the beard has gone at any rate.'

'Do you miss it?'

'I prefer you like this. I can see more of your gorgeous face.'

'Maybe I can grow it for next year. And find a Santa costume that actually fits.'

'Ooh yes! And I'll dress up as Mrs Claus and Shona can be an elf. We can do it in November – it can be our Christmas card.'

He shook his head but couldn't stop the laugh from escaping. 'I see you've rediscovered your love of Christmas.'

'Yes, I think I have,' she replied. 'But now it's even more exciting because we can make it special for Shona.'

THAT AFTERNOON, SITTING AROUND THE TABLE IN THE dining room, Rory knew he'd made his peace with Christmas and being a father. He was wearing a paper hat and sharing cracker jokes with Brad as everyone else laughed at the terrible jokes. His mother's sharp edges had been smoothed by copious amounts of Morag's sloe gin, and she appeared besotted with her granddaughter. Shona didn't seem fazed by the noise or being passed around for cuddles, and Zoe couldn't stop smiling. He felt her happiness filling every part of him. They were full of good food and surrounded by their family and friends. Even his best mate, Charlie, had joined them for a chat from Columbia with the whole of Valentina's family yelling in the background and demanding to see the baby.

After lunch, they relaxed in the library in front of a roaring fire. Brad wheeled in a massive TV, and they all watched *A Muppet Christmas Carol*, which had just nudged ahead of *Die Hard* in a vote they'd had earlier for the best Christmas film. Afterwards, Jamie got out his guitar and he and Sam took requests. It was perfect.

❦

JANUARY 1st

RORY: *HAPPY NEW YEAR EVERYONE FROM ALL OF US.*

TABI: *It's not New Year yet.*

RORY: *It is on this side of the pond. You keep playing catch up, Aganos.*

BEN: *Happy New Year from me and Laurie in Somerset!*

SABRINA: *It could be news year I not sure as I have been drinking fpr a few hours.*

TABI: *It's drunk Sabrina! I miss drunk Sabrina.*

TRISTAN: *I blame Sherilyn. She brought some kind of Kentucky home brew to the party. I've either lost the enamel on my teeth or the lining of my stomach.*

SABRINA: *Chicagooooo! It's my kinda tooooooooooooown.*

BEN: *I can't believe we're going to see you all in seven months. Laurie's never been to America before.*

TRISTAN: *It's going to be the wedding of the year!*

JONATHAN: *Yay! And guess who's going to be the best man?*

JONATHAN: *Me!*

SABRINA: *That's so lovleeee! Tris, why dinn't you tell me?*

TRISTAN: *We can actually talk, Bree. I'm only on the other side of the room.*

RORY: *Can someone remind me why I agreed to bring my wife and daughter to Kentucky for Tristan's wedding?*

JONATHAN: *It's because I have one of the most advanced tractors in the world - the John Deere 9RX 640 and you want a go.*

RORY: *Ah yes.*

TABI: *Jonathan, has your wife agreed to let Rory ride your tractor? I didn't know you had an open marriage.*

RORY: *Sigh.*

TABI: You'd better buckle up tight, Bagpipes. I've heard that Jonathan's got a beast.

RORY: Right. I'm going to bugger off and spend time with the two most amazing women in the world. See you in July...

The end. Or is it...

❧ II ❧
NO CRIB AND NO BED

By
Kelly Kay

PROLOGUE

February 12 – Chicago, IL
United Lounge, O'Hare Airport
4:46 p.m. CST

TABI

Last call.

Everyone is fucking crazy right now, and I love it. We just finished up a dance party and everyone was making a complete ass of themselves except grumpy Haggis breath who sat and watched. Sabrina and Jonathan stopped using glasses like a half hour ago and just passed a bottle. Tristan actually unbuttoned his vest and danced with the rest of us to some old-school hip hop. He knew every word. Ben is flailing his hands in the air as I make my way over to the corner of the room where we spent most of our time. The lounge and flight crews got quite a show. They stayed in their corner of the world behind some glass, but we were like a fish tank for them. I never care who's watching or what's being said. It's the gift of no filter—or that the appearance of no filter or not caring is a powerful shield.

We're packing up our belongings to head to our gates. The lights are on everywhere, not just in our oasis. I look around and suddenly I'm going to miss these people. I don't usually bond well. Ask any of my female friends. Poppy Gelbert once said I wasn't a hand holding friend. And I've known her since she was born. I feel a kinship with her cousin, Rebecca, she's not much of a girl's girl either, but Becca's brother, David, is like a blood bond to me. I hold David's hand all the time. Not sure what it is about women that I don't connect with as deeply, but men on a deep friendship level have always been easier for me.

Sabrina's fantastic, though, and I hope we stay connected. She's spirited, goofy, and also holds the right amount of cynicism. As soon as she gets out of her own way, she'll be fine. This blind date tomorrow is probably a tremendous mistake, but she'll figure it out.

I feel the same affection and trust towards these idiots I've known for six hours as I do to some of my lifelong friends at home. I don't know what magic was in this bubble of time but I'm here for it.

I start clearing up our discarded wine bottles and old plates of cheese. There are quite a lot. I can feel the mountain that is Rory behind me. I flip around with a half-drunk bottle and offer it to him. "Not too late for a nip there, Kilt."

He shakes his head.

His blond hair is falling around his shoulders and his massive tree-trunk arms are crossed over his chest. Thor comes to mind. I should get him a hammer. Someone must have already done that. "Hey, does Zoe make you play super-heroes in bed?"

He shakes his head, then a serious look falls over his face. He says, "I see you. And I'm not that observant of a person."

I shake him off and turn back to loading my bag. I'll miss these people, but I also like that they only get a piece of me. Rory's stare makes me feel like he sees too much.

"The lady doth protest too much." He steps closer.

I turn around, put my hands on my hips and roll my eyes. "About what? And don't forget, I'm not much of a lady."

"Kids."

He knocks the wind out of me, and I can't stop my emotions from climbing onto my face and into my eyes. Shit. I turn away to compose myself and tuck away my dirty secret.

He speaks again, "And you're not drunk."

I can handle that revelation. "No. When wine is what you teethe on, it takes enough to drown an elephant for me to get wine drunk. I could drink it all day long and still do something intricate and complicated at the end of the day."

Rory scoffs and kinda cracks a smile, I can't really tell.

"If you want to see all this crazy get drunk, pour me tequila. I can handle maybe one shot. Vodka, one cocktail and bourbon, now there's a swift, warm and yummy drunk, but no. I'm not currently buzzed."

"And you're not pregnant."

That's a little harsher than the man realizes and I'm not sure how the hell he sees that, but ok. I'll bite. His eyes are softened from his usually steely glare and there's a kinship connection. His sincerity knocks me back and my suspicion is, no one *really* knows him either. I'm going to guess Zoe is pretty fucking fantastic and that Rory and Bax would get along a scary amount.

I grin and it comes out a little strained and sad. I'm honest this time. "I only do that for a month or so at a time. Then suddenly I'm not pregnant. Then there's long stretches of needles, vitamins, acupuncture and odd Greek rituals performed by annoying cousins who think fertility is something that can be fixed. It can't. We're working on other things. I'm ok."

"You're not." He's quick.

"No. I'm not." I'm honest.

There's a pause and I shake it off as Sabrina stumbles to us. She's followed by everyone else in their own drunken gaits, all preparing to scurry off to their individual gates that will take them to either the places they're from, the places they'll be from or, in Sabrina's case, to a man she's never seen who's named after a penis.

"You throw the best, I mean, *the* best parties, Tabi!" She tumbles and Rory catches her. She laughs and Jonathan stumbles back to us as well. Rory looks over the top of Sabrina's head.

He speaks, knowing no one else in the room will understand him. And maybe that's the thing about this weird-as-shit bond between us, often no one in the room understands me. And I would bet all the wine these assholes drank, it's the same for him.

"You're not ok, but you will be."

I nod curtly to stop myself from becoming vulnerable and sobbing. I smile and turn towards Tristan who throws an arm around me.

"Tabitha, darling. I had a shit couple of days in your country, but I leave here, schnocked, happy and hopeful. You did that. And I thank you," Tristan says while swaying.

I want him to be happy and the tale of the half torso perfect women doesn't seem to be over yet. "Listen, Tris, you don't know all the shit she's hiding yet, but don't hide too. Do I need to straighten her out as well as Jonathan's long-lost love?"

He laughs heartily and squeezes my shoulder, then kisses me on the cheek. "I have it well in hand. Or I will. You're right. I'm not quite done with Sherilyn yet."

I turn and embrace him fully, and he walks towards Rory.

Ben shakes Rory's hand. "Mate."

Rory semi smiles. "You'll do great. The company is going to be a success, you'll turn it around."

Ben smiles. "Thanks. And I hope I find someone like your Zoe someday."

Rory says, "Trust me, there's no one like my Zoe. But someday I do hope it's as jarring and sudden for you as it was for me." He slaps Ben on the back and turns to Tristan.

Jonathan gives me a huge sloppy hug and it's kind of like being squeezed by an octopus crossed with a Buick and a golden retriever.

"She'll love me, right?" He breaks my heart He's such a sweetie, but a little dopey and too trusting. We all know he's making a tremendous mistake, but he needs to see it for himself before I can really help him out. I just gave fate a little nudge, the rest is up to him.

I say, "Get your head out of your crop and fix your fucking life, you hear me? I know a thing or two about being obsessed with soil, yields and harvest."

His giant blue eyes open to me even wider. "You do! You're a farmer."

"At the core of who I am, I'm a farmer. I just have a better tasting crop than most."

He laughs. "I'll send you some whiskey if they use my wheat, and we can compare."

And that's when they'll see me drunk, one sip of his whiskey and I'll be gone. But I'll bet he'll be sober. Will be a nice role reversal for him.

I grin, knowing he'll never remember I called his ex and

told her to get her ass in gear. I hope she listens. I hope I don't have to fly to get her and drag her down to Kentucky to make sure this gentle, fabulous giant doesn't marry that horrible woman.

Sabrina flings herself at Rory and squeals, "You're all so tall. You're tall and handsome. I want a tall and handsome. Not you but someone."

He kisses her on the top of her head, and I'm shocked at his affection. Then he pulls way back and grabs his things roughly as if that will negate the moment. I'm guessing he's afraid to be a dad. I know the type. But he's got it down pat.

I turn back to Rory and catch his eye. We don't hug or give platitudes about everything happening for a reason. I simply say, "I see you too, Kilt. And you'll be fine."

Sonoma, CA
December 23, 11:58 pm PST
Prohibition Winery

BAX

I watch my wife pull her coat around her as a December wind kicks up. Her ebony hair is so long now it whips around her head like a swarm of bees. Her long hair is the only outward sign of her pain or that anything is wrong. No one notices. That's who she is to almost everyone, except me. Carefree, wild, brash and brave. But I know her better than anyone and I feel it all with and for her. If I could take this frustration, fear and pain from her I would. I'd bear the burden for both of us. But apparently there's only so much we can do. And that might be the hardest part for Tabi.

She's an action girl believing there's always a solution, a way forward. She gets results instantly or figures out a way to fix everything. She barrels through life righting the wrongs and injustices of the world or for her friends. Hell, she's inserted herself into five virtual strangers' lives in the past year. Random people she met at an airport, and they all think they're better off for her meddling. She sees things clearly and knows how to fix them, always has.

The irony is fertility isn't like that. It's not linear, it doesn't make sense and often no one can point to a cause, so she feels the effects of what she thinks is failure, deeply. The miscarriages were bad, but losing the foster boys was worse. We knew them and loved them.

We've stopped the shots and are coming to terms with her hormones as they cascade down to normal from fucking crazy when she was shooting up.

I suspect her dad feels the depth of it with her, they're too similar for him to miss it. Both annoyingly obstinate, so dialed into each other it borders on psychic. But she can't fix this no matter how hard she tries. She has to stop throwing herself into the shots, vitamins, acupuncture, yoga, worldwide adoption papers, the foster parenting, and accept we are unable to find a solution.

So, it's just us. And thank God for each other. If I get to walk the world for another hundred years with only one person, it damn well better be the bright-ass insane shooting star, my Bee.

We're going away early on Christmas morning because we can't bear a massive 5 Families holiday with tons of kids running around. There are five winery families here in Sonoma that make up most of our world. Our immediate families are two of them, but we were raised in the "village" that is ever-expanding.

Our parents were angry, but I convinced them this was an adventure we wanted to take, not that we couldn't handle being around our pregnant friends and our parents' sad looks.

We simply said we wanted to go somewhere warm and have a different kind of Christmas this year. We're packed and ready to get out of here for three weeks to Brazil. Somewhere we've never been and never thought we'd go, but anywhere but here sounded fucking perfect.

Sam Langerford, David Gelbert and Josh Whittier are our best friends and business partners. We've all known each other since about birth when our parents decided to become best friends and take us along for the ride. David and Josh's kids, respectively, are already forming the third generation's bond. Something that pulls at both of us and we're trying to overcome.

We love being Aunt Tabi and Uncle Bax to blood relatives and our extended "family" but right now we need to be away from it. My sister and her wife's egg was fertilized the first time they did IUI. We've been very unsuccessful with that little procedure. And a complete failure with way too many fucking cycles of IVF and with two miscarriages, we're fucking done. If our kid is out there in the universe somewhere, I wish they'd show up or let us stop hoping.

Tabi usually keeps her hair short, just below her ears in a bob so it doesn't annoy her when she's out with the vines. But she stopped caring about it when our foster boys went back to their mother in the fall. The hard part was having to convince them to leave us. That their crackhead mom cared about them instead of the larger welfare check. Fucking stung like a jellyfish lashed at my insides.

I flip the bright twinkle lights off and tug on the tasting room door of Prohibition Winery to make sure it's locked. Our winery had a big sales day. Well, it's ours and our three best friends. I'm only here part time, but it's Tabi's whole life.

She's walking the driveway towards our house which sits on the edge our winery. The house she loves, and I fucking detest.

She insisted we renovate this dilapidated piece-of-shit farm-house that was on the winery property when we all bought it. We own the land on the boundary of the vineyard, so the structure looks like it's on the property, but it's ours. The five of us own the vineyard in equal parts. But this fucking house, Jesus, I hate it. Every time we get a piece of it done, another falls apart. It's cursed even though she says it's lucky. I loathe our home but love her.

Only Tabi Aganos could think that because the house falls apart it safeguards us from evil things. She may not carry on a lot of her mother's Greek orthodox traditions but irrational belief in evil spirits and luck is one of them. She and her mother actually had a cleansing ceremony for her womb. Her aunts and cousins flew in from Greece to bring special shit to burn. The house smelled like charred octopus and burnt pencil erasers for a week. The results were inconclusive, according to Tab.

She stops halfway up to our house, passing the dormant Zinfandel vines that are brown and twisted like a mass of rubber bands in a drawer. She glances over at the large, reno-vated barn that houses our new, shiny admin offices with a full basketball court out front. There's an equipment barn back on the property. And this one attaches to another large barn structure that houses our steel tanks, enology lab, and the empty barrels before they get filled. Our crush pad is in there as well. It's where you find Sam, Tabi and David most days. The three of them do the bulk of Prohibition's work while Josh manages his family vineyard with his dad, and I run the city of Sonoma most days.

Eventually the back barn will be a couple of sleeping quar-ters for extra help we bring on for harvest. It's simply a couple of giant empty rooms waiting to be filled next fall.

This year will be our first full harvest of our own grapes.

We'll buy a little juice from all our families' wineries. We each have one that our parents still run. But that juice is mostly for nostalgia from how this place began. We do a limited run of "Pro/Ho Saved My Ass" blend each year for our original wine club members, to continue to say thank you. My mind drifts to that story for a second and I smile at how far Prohibition has come. I hear her throaty, loud voice over the distance and wind.

"Bax, why are there lights on in my barn?"

I yell back as I approach her, "First off, it's not your barn. It's all of ours. And second, I think David and Josh are buffing the floor or something."

She fires back as I get closer to her, "Are we sure they're not buffing each other?"

I roll my eyes while she laughs at her own juvenile joke and pull her towards me. It's been a shitty year, and I couldn't love her more. I've loved her since we were five, and it's scary that with each day, I seriously love this brash, outrageous, ridiculous woman even more. She throws her arms around me, and I push her hair from her face. Her coffee eyes taking in my expression.

She says, "Wasn't Sam supposed to do that? The buffing. He's the one putting a fucking gym in the back of the front barn."

Ever since our friend, Sam, was ghosted by the love of his life, he found a new religion in becoming, for lack of a better word, buff. He's a meathead manwhore now, and we're all adjusting to his new norm. We all miss his ex-girlfriend, Sammy, but he thinks that if he can lift enough weight or fuck enough strangers, he can forget her. So far, he's just become a bit of an asshole and is no closer to closure. I miss our chubby, positive teddy bear of a reliable friend. The one we all opened up to simply when he'd hug us. But we've all been through stages of assholery and life experimentation, now it's his turn, so we endure it. But we can't wait until he gets back to being himself again or at least onto his next enlightened plane of existence.

I tell her, "Sam's at dinner with his parents, then has a date or two later."

"I thought I crushed some ass in my lifetime. And David was a hall of famer, but it's like Sam's possessed to out-fuck us all." I grin as she says, "Are the women folk in there with them buffing?"

David's wife dragged Josh's fiancée out tonight to spite her husband. "Nat and Elle went into San Francisco with all the little girls to see *The Nutcracker* because David went with his mom the other night and wouldn't take Nat with him."

"Seriously, he wouldn't take his wife to the ballet?"

"Tradition." I shrug.

"But it's *The Nutcracker*, well, I mean—"

"Please no jokes about how that's your new nickname."

She laughs, then opens her mouth to speak again. I silence her with a kiss. My soul flames as her lips meet mine. She's not one for light, gentle kisses, but that's what I'm aiming for.

I'm the only one who gets to control, stop, command or understand her at any one time. I bask in that role. She's the only one who ever saw me as more than what was expected of me. She's always been the spark to my life and I'm her counter-balance.

I brush my lips along hers, then move down towards her jaw. I nip at it, and she throws her head back. "Be with me, Tab. Close your brain for the night. I have ideas for you."

She moans my favorite sound in the world. We haven't had non-fertility sex in a while. Free, unscheduled non-ovulation sex. I long to bend her over couches and fuck her on our very expensive, newly renovated for the third time, kitchen counters. Water and plumbing destroyed the first kitchen, an electrical fire took out the second. She keeps saying the third one is lucky. She's more hopeful than I am.

I'm slowly coming to terms with the fact that it might be just us. There are worse things than spending the rest of my life basking in her glorious chaos. I'm mayor of Sonoma, for now, and I feel like I'm finally in service the way I'm supposed to be. And Pro/Ho finally turned a profit. Our families are healthy, Josh's mom's Parkinson's seems to be at bay for the moment and everyone except Sam is happy. And everyone we've ever met can get pregnant just by looking at their partner except us. I need to close my brain tonight too.

I crush my mouth to hers and it's met with her glorious, aggressive tongue. Our teeth are gnashing and clicking as we try to get closer. Her hand moves down my body and underneath my long farmer's coat. It rests on her favorite toy.

"Looks like the Senator is up." My dick is harder than it should be out in the open, but that's what she does to me. Every fucking time.

I flip her around to face our house, pinning her back to my front with my forearm against her chest. I pinch her ear between my teeth and rasp. "This is what's going to happen." She gasps. It's been a while since I took complete control of her, and I'm desperate for it. And I think she's desperate to let go.

"We're going into the house and you're going to lose all these clothes. Then you're going to remove mine, take my cock out and place it between those naturally full and reddish lips of yours and suck. Swallow me down until I hit the back of your throat and get to fuck your stunning face, until I'm about to spill. Then I'll take your sexy ass upstairs and eat your pussy until you're about to explode. At that time, I'll flip over, and you get to ride me until my dick fills you so completely you can't fucking speak. Ride so hard your tits can't keep up with your hips unless I grab them and hold them hard. You get to come over and over. And I may finish between those tits or your ass. Not sure yet." She's breathing heavily, and my dick is ready to punch through my jeans and find the first available hole.

She rounds on me quickly, her eyes hooded and sharp. "I love a good plan. Race you." She turns again towards the house. I smack her full, lush ass with a pointed sting. She yelps, then moans and runs towards the house. I follow quickly, making sure to unzip my coat. She's shedding clothes as she goes. I pass her jacket and as lust-filled as I am, I just can't leave it there. I pick it up. Then her sweater and her bra. She turns around and she's topless on our porch. Fuck, her tits are perfect. Her large brown nipples are peaked and so hard in the chill of the evening. I want to bury myself in them. I want to fuck them until dawn. God, I want her. Thank fucking God she's my wife and I get to do this anytime.

She cocks a hip when I get to the base of the porch stairs. "Did you just pick up my clothes?" I throw them in the house. "You didn't have to pick up after me."

I shrug. "It's what I do."

She grins. "Let's get to the rest of what you're going to do..."

❧ II ❧

TABI

His cock is my favorite. I've done the research; I used to have a list. But his, by far, is the biggest and most attractive cock in the world. Sometimes I wish I could share it with people, so they'd understand how under-privileged they are. I've discussed it with Sam's brother and his husband, but they don't actually get the full scope of how insanely attractive The Senator is without pictures. And it's the one line he's specifically asked me not to cross. I'm kind of proud I've never shown his dick to anyone. I can play by the rules, despite what people think.

We were about to get to the spanking part when he got an emergency city call, so I'm sitting on our makeshift living room furniture. The leftovers from both of our old houses. I hate this furniture because it's not ours. It's mine or it was his. And his ex sat on his favorite chair at one point, and I do not care for that bitch at all.

I'm sure the city's emergency is something stupid. An alarm

went off at the community center and they can't remember where the box is to shut it off. Or possibly the asshole barista's kid, found more spray paint and decorated the sidewalk in front of Reader's Books with balls again. That kid needs a book and a hobby. He's interrupted my sex life too often. I cross my legs as Bax drifts in the room stroking his dick while he's on the phone. That's hot. He points to me and gestures for me to open my legs. He grins and licks his lips, then points for me to go upstairs. I raise a finger to him.

He says gruffly into the phone, "What? No. Don't do that." He turns away as he looks for a pen and paper. I toss on his t-shirt and search for my phone to plug in but discover a text.

RORY: Christ. Are you there?

Usually, I'd tune out my phone in my current situation. But I've grown too close to these people. They've been my respite from my intense and large extended family all around me. And only one of them knows what the last year has truly been for me. Everyone else on the planet's pregnancy and kids bug the shit out of me, but not him for some odd reason. Maybe because he has yet to see it for the joy that it is and is bogged down in the worry part. It's fucking funny to hear him squirm and be uncomfortable. I kind of live for it lately.

TABI: About to fuck my husband, super dirty and nasty, but I've got a second.

RORY: Stop. That poor man. Does he know what he's getting?

TABI: What's wrong?

RORY: She and Brad are bloody holding some kind of fucking ceremony with white robes and shite.

TABI: And?

RORY: I'm sitting at our pediatrician's appointment and apparently the buggered ritual still has an hour left. Because the bloody fucking candle hasn't crackled yet. What the fuck? My girl is too small to be subjected to Pop-Pop Brad.

TABI: Look, you can't rush a good candle crackling. Go get a biscuit and chill. She'll be fine.

RORY: She won't be fine unless a doctor sees her.

TABI: Are there issues?

RORY: NO! But medical professionals should be taking care of Zoe and Shona not a self-appointed, self-involved, mother-stealing druid high priest bullshit Shaman! It's a baby who needs to be medically looked after not chanted at.

Bax sees me texting and his eyes flair. It's sexy, but I can tell he's a little mad. He scribbles on a piece of paper.

GET YOUR ASS TO OUR BED. LEAVE THE PHONE. RORY CAN WAIT UNTIL LATER TO FREAK OUT. I NEED TO FUCK YOUR TITS. TAKE MY SHIRT OFF.

I quickly text.

TABI: I have to go. Apparently, my tits have a date with my husband's dick.

RORY: No. Just no. Stop. Go. Kill me.

I remove Bax's shirt and walk up behind him. I press into his back and reach around. The Senator's not as stiff as he was but grows instantly at my touch. He's still talking, and I start moving my hand up and back along his shaft. He turns around to me and mouths the word, "GO," pointing to our staircase that's seen better days. It's the next thing we're going to replace. The stairs are uneven, they're stable, but have different pitches as you go up as if someone just randomly put boards together in a stair pattern. And the banister is splinter central.

But the kitchen and bathrooms are perfection. We salvaged the old iron clawfoot tub for our bathroom. And we have the biggest most luxurious bed. Solid walnut, tall with four sturdy posts we use for various activities. If there are ever kids, they'll need a stepladder and a probably a key to get in the door.

Bax had the bed made for me. It's a replica from a Kansas

B&B we stayed in ages ago. Before we knew we were Tabi and Bax. Well, we were ignoring the fact that we were written in the stars. We trashed that room, wrecked that bed, and I puked most of the night. But he remembered all the same details I did from that bed. That bed was the first time we truly made love, and we didn't even call it that.

They had to finish constructing the bed in the room because it was too heavy to take up the fucked-up staircase all at once. It was then and there I decided we're never moving because I couldn't bear to leave the bed.

Bax wraps me in his arms. It's a little sexy but way too soft. He's pointing to the steps, and I just bite my lip and stare at him. He's gotten back to the gym lately with Sam and Josh. He was never out of shape, but now he's got all these abs popping and biceps I want to bite. And that beautiful V is more defined and sexier. It's like his hips are notched. His sprinkle of blond all around the perfect dick matches the hair on his head. His intense blue eyes are in overdrive right now. Damn. I mean, there's not a pussy in the world that wouldn't weep for him.

"Sup? Senator not into this anymore?" My nickname for his dick since we were twenty years old. He's always a stand-up guy, does the right thing and he's not afraid of hard work. Just like Bax.

He tosses his phone and grabs his dick. "I have to go there's something brewing at the police station, but I think we might just have time for a session of congress."

He's taken to calling my pussy the speaker of the house. "Joint Session of Congress" is our way of saying we want to leave and fuck when we're in the company of the increasing number of children our friends are having. If our friends get it, they don't comment. Probably because they're knee-deep in sippy cups and apple sauce packets.

He squeezes my backside, and I kiss him. I dance my lips

over this man, like I've done thousands of times and it's always butterflies. Always fireworks and goosebumps exploding on my skin because of Bax.

I get bored easily. I get tired of clothing all the time. Literally just donate something I'm wearing because I can't stand the sight of it any longer. I tire of the 5 and their spouses when I'm around them too much. Like right now I can't stand Sam. And the Airport Lounge Five are fabulous because it's like I'm invested in my life, but I have them on the side. I get annoyed quickly, then have to walk away and regroup in meetings or with my family. But somehow, Bax has defied all Tabi logic and reason. He rises above all the noise and apathy. I miss him every second I'm not around him and get excited when we reunite, even if he's just run out to Whole Foods. And he feels that too.

Perhaps that's the secret to marriage, meeting each other at the same level of excitement and the same level of sorrow. We fought more in the last year doing all this fertility bullshit than we ever have. But we're aware it comes from the frustration of banging our heads against a wall. We're like my fellow Greek, Sisyphus, the boulder keeps rolling right over us just when we get to the top, but now it's time to get out of the way.

When we fight—I fight dirty, he fights way too fair and logically—it always settles, and we figure out why. And I'd like it said for the record, it's not always my fault.

This kiss is getting heated as I rake my hands through his hair. My phone signals a text. He growls against my lips but I nibble the bottom of his. I'd never answer it now, not on the verge of a multiple mind-blowing orgasms. The man rocks it every time and somehow, I swear to God, it gets hotter and better. I'm dripping in anticipation of this man taking me however he wants. He glides over my body and down my hips. He skates his fingers through my wetness in search of one of his favorite things. Then, without warning, he finds his way inside me easily. I gasp and he uses two fingers, pumping in and out of me slowly while I kiss him. I hear his phone ring. We ignore it. The city can burn for all I fucking care.

My phone dings again, and he removes his fingers. I don't like it, but then he bends down and hoists my naked body over his. Then he bites my ass. I squeal.

"Dude, your chest is going to get awfully wet this way." I reach down and smack his ass. He grunts and starts for our rickety steps. Both our phones are going crazy but all that matters is us.

The floors groan. I love the sound of this ridiculously creaky house. Bax would love to build from scratch, salt the earth of this place, but the history and feel of it are too rich and wonderful to get rid of. And he bought it for me. He envisioned a life here beyond anything I'd ever dreamed of. We share the property with Pro/Ho, and I can walk to the work that fills my soul. There's no other place I'd rather be than on this property.

He throws me onto the bed, well, maybe this is the place I'd rather be.

He strokes the Senator and I sigh. This all started out dirty but the look in his eyes says this is going to end up sweeter and more meaningful than just fucking. I adore all shades of sex with Bax. He lies on top of me, lining up perfectly. I treasure the weight of this man on top. I'm protected and safe, even from myself, when he's in this position.

"I love you, Bee," he says.

"I know," I say.

"No. You don't. There's no way you could possibly understand."

"I take great offense to that—" And I lose my words as he calls the Joint Session of Congress to order with a stiff gavel.

He's so familiar and new. I moan loudly. And he looks at me. He moves slightly and I bring my hips to his. We crest and I arch my back. He's sliding in and out of me so easily. It has the right amount of tension and roll to it. Oh god, he's fucking good at fucking.

Bax whispers on my lips, "Hang on, my love. I've been thinking about fucking you hard all day."

I grin and a wicked little smile overtakes his beautiful face. His blue eyes gleam in the dark as I comb through his blond hair. He's due for a haircut, it's longer than he likes it but still Boy Scout appropriate. He backs out of me, and I groan.

"No worries. I'll be right back. Just need you in a little bit of a different position."

I sit up and he slowly pushes me back.

"Arms above your head and leave them there. I like when your tits move with us." He leans down and slides each nipple through his teeth. It's almost too much. Then he's between my legs and says, "You're soaking for me. Someone wants it hard as well." I moan in approval. He stretches me open and laps up all he can, then sucks hard on my clit.

I whine, "Bax."

He loves holding me off and making me beg. I'm at his complete mercy as his tongue swirls on my clit. I want to move my hands, but I don't. He works me until I'm panting and writhing on his face.

"Oh, fuck. When are you going to fuck me hard? Just curious how long I have to keep enduring this edging."

He looks up at me and wipes his face. He quickly leans down and spears his tongue into my mouth. He controls all of this and all of me in these moments. I surrender.

He moves back down my body and then one leg is on his shoulder, the other bent and in the crook of his arm. His cock is so big that I will never truly be prepared when he takes me like this. He slams into me and my tits indeed bounce for him. His eyes are fixated on where we join. And I clench him tight.

"FUCK. That's good." And then he pulls out and slams back into me harder. I'm so full of this man and he's possessed. His pace picks up and my other leg finds its way to his shoulder and his hands to my hips. He's pulling me onto him, and I can do nothing but moan and hold onto the sheets around me. I'm careful to let my tits still bounce for him. We're loud and the slapping of our skin is echoing through our room. It's hot and rough. We haven't played like this in ages but we both really need to let loose. I'm on fire, about to explode again. His face is so intense, and his muscles are contracting as he fucks me even harder. He sees me watching us and I pinch a nipple for him. He throws his head back and forward almost thrashing. The intensity of his stare could cut glass. He's so hard slamming into me, filling me. I feel him bottom out, and I can't take it anymore and moan his name loudly.

"Fuck, Tab. I have to come."

"Me first. Me first," I scream. He groans but doesn't stop his pace. He reaches down and works my clit. My hands fly to my breasts as I knead and pull them.

"Yes, play with your tits. Jesus, you know how hot that makes me."

And then I'm there.

"I'm coming. I'm coming. Right fucking now." It spirals and I clench and hold him in deeper, if that's even possible. Fuck. My whole body lifts off the bed, and I swear to God, I'm floating above us. Stars slam my eyes closed as I groan the last bits of my orgasm.

I can't come down. I'm so sensitive and then he's at it. I notice, now I'm post coming, our bed is rocking. He's pulled me to the bottom of our bed and he's standing and giving it to me even harder. Our heavy wooden bed is no match for Bax's pounding. It creaks and slams into the wall. I love it all. And then he lowers my legs and yells my name. He thrusts into me until he's emptied himself. He moans and leans down kissing me tenderly. He looks like the boy I fell in love with decades ago. Every day, I still can't believe I get to have him.

BAX

That was some world-class fucking. Maybe because we did it just to feel good. I kiss her again. "Too much?"

She grins. "Never."

I leave my favorite place with a groan. We seriously just hard fucked for like an hour. I'm not sure where my stamina came from, but I couldn't stop.

"Don't move." I run into the bathroom and grab a washcloth to clean her. I hear our phones downstairs and dread finding them. I look at her from the door of the bedroom.

She sits up on her elbows. "Do it. Leap to me!"

I laugh and, as always, do as Tabi commands. I put one foot back and she giggles. The house is making all its old house noises, and I sigh.

She scolds. "It's just saying hello."

"No. It's probably something in the walls that's growing

and eating away at the roof or something. That's the one thing we've only replaced once."

"Be nice to the house."

I take off running and leap onto the bed, then stand quickly. I jump into the air and land with a thud on our matress. The house groans again. I clean us off and toss the towel into our hamper. And our hamper sinks a tiny bit. I sit up next to her.

"Tab, I must be tired. Our hamper just creaked and started to slide—"

Suddenly there's a loud crack like lightning, followed by our hamper falling through the floor.

"What the fuck?" She sits up and we look at each other.

Then there's a louder clap that could be thunder and without warning our bed begins to sink through the floor. I clasp the headboard and haul her into my arms, then without another warning we crash through the floor down into our dining room and into the ceiling of the basement.

I turn to her, panicked. And she mutters, "I'm ok. You?"

"I am." We both feel each other's bodies frantically to make sure the other person is really alright.

Perhaps after the shock wears off, we'll be hurt, but I feel fine. I don't know how I'm getting out of here. The impact of the crash didn't feel as if I broke anything. Aside from the splintered wood from the ceiling and floor joists, and the dust everywhere, our bed is unscathed. I look up at the hole into our bedroom and the dresser begins to move and falls through the hole next to us making the first floor/basement ceiling a bit more unstable.

We're about two feet down into the basement and I'm afraid if we move the bed will fall further. And then, without any ceremony or creaking, her motherfucking iron bathtub falls through the kitchen ceiling destroying our thrice-made custom countertops.

I look to her and she's stifling a laugh. I glare at her. "HOLY FUCKING CHRIST, I HATE THIS HOUSE." And then she full-on belly laughs as do I. We're hysterically laughing. I can't breathe. She can't speak. I'm bent in half when we hear Josh screaming to David. Thank God they were working on the barns. They're on the front porch.

Josh bellows. He has a commanding voice, and I can tell he's scared shitless. "Shit! Are you guys in there? BAX! TABITHA! Answer me right now!!"

I yell, "WE'RE FINE. WE'RE IN THE FLOOR." And another bout of inappropriate hysterical laughing breaks out.

"I can hear them. I think they're laughing." David opens the front door, and I pull the sheet over Tabi.

"Holy fuck." David says as they walk gingerly over to us.

"Sup, assholes?" my darling wife says.

David asks, "Did you fuck a hole in your floor?"

Josh yells, "Are you hurt, you lunatics?"

David runs a hand over his shorn red hair and scratches his chin like he's feeling for a beard. He grows them during harvest and shaves when the last grape is crushed. David's built like a lean muscular basketball player. Josh has more of a wide, tall build. They might be able to help us out of this. Ironically, we need Sam now that he's huge and buff.

All our phones go off at once. Mine is hanging near the edge of the hole and Tabi's is on the ruined couch that's covered in debris. David silences his and Josh ignores it.

"Bax, it seems we have to get you out of here without you falling further."

Tabi looks at Josh. "Yeah. Seems like it. Get me the fuck out of the floor." Her sheet falls a bit and Josh looks away. David shrugs.

Tabi turns to me. "What? He's seen them. You've all seen them. No big." She used to enjoy creeping us all out by flashing us. I only pretended that it was gross.

My voice is a bit rough. "Yes. But they're mine now and I'd appreciate if no one else saw them."

"But they're so good." Tabi is rightly proud of her boobs.

Josh and David nod and my ginger friend says, "She's right. They are good."

"Thanks, David."

I yell, "Enough about her tits. Get us out of here. Josh, throw me your hoodie."

He pulls it off and tosses it to us. I put it over Tabi's head, it will hang to her mid-thigh. That's good. Well, it's better.

Josh and David are about three feet from the bed and the giant hole in the floor of the first floor. It could all blow.

"I'll call Matteo, he was working late on your sister's construction project." Josh walks out to the front porch to call our remarkably busy contractor and our phones pop off again.

Tabi says, "David, can you see if that's for all of us? Like is one of our parents dead or a wildfire? No one could know about this shitshow here."

David pulls his phone out. "It's just Becca." Him blowing off his sister isn't new.

I offer up, "There's no way she's calling all of us so something else is going on."

Josh reenters. "Ok. So. Matteo is on his way with a couple of guys, and he's warned David and I to get out of the house." He's our contractor and builder for all of Pro/Ho and is currently building out some buildings on my family winery and for my sister's recording studio project. And he keeps warning us this fucking house isn't worth the effort and money. He also said it's barely making code.

"Are you fucking kidding me? Get Sam over here. He'll

brute this thing out." She moves a bit too much and the bed, or the floor, or the house creaks.

"Stop gesturing," I say calmly.

"I'm Greek. That's impossible."

"I don't want to die because you had to talk with your hands."

David says, "Seems fair." Both he and Josh are on the porch. The structure I thought we'd fall through first, but it seems to be standing. I'm terrified of the roof caving in on us. I don't know how to fix this or protect her. I'm no good if I can't protect her.

"Josh. Get us the fuck out of here. Screw Matteo. Get her out." Josh doesn't question me; he's as protective as I am. Well, he's over the top insane with it, but he gets me.

David tries to stop him. "They're fine. We don't want to do any more damage. Just wait."

Josh shakes him off and David throws his hands in the air. I hear a truck pull up. I yell, "Who's that?"

David smiles. "The crown prince of assholery has arrived. Everyone step aside."

Tabi says, "He's our resident douchenozzle now you've laid down your crown."

David replies, "You take that back or I'll pull out some old dickish moves. Pick a fight or something."

I yell, "Again. Focus."

Sam bounds up the stairs and fills the doorway. Seriously when you take a teddy bear and turn him into a grizzly it's miraculous. He's honestly filling the doorframe.

"Why the fuck aren't you assholes answering your phones? I had to literally stop fingering a chick so I could deliver—" He stops talking when he sees Tabi and me.

Tabi yells, "GET ME OUT!"

Sam appraises the situation. "Did you fuck a hole in the floor?"

David slaps him on his chest. "That's what I said." He high-fives him.

Josh says, "Jag offs. Listen up. David, run and get rope from the barn. We'll tie it to the front of Sam's truck and to the bed." They look over at us.

David grins. "You cool with tying stuff to the bed? I know that used to be on Tabi's fuck-it list but has that skill tarnished? How are your knots these days?"

Sam laughs. "Seriously. You're worried about knot tying when I'm here." We all laugh. Sam loves a good Shibari knot.

Tabi shouts at him, "How are your knots these days, big guy?"

Sam bristles and shoots back, "Don't you fucking worry about my skills."

Sam put all of it in the past when his girlfriend ghosted him. But they were the perfect BDSM couple. It's nice to hear a bit of the old Sam joke with us.

Josh slaps him on the back. They used to be insanely close. But then Josh has had kids nonstop since he met Elle, and Sam, well, he changed.

TABI

The boys are all discussing where to put the ropes and whatnot, and they're driving me insane. I'm itchy and nervous. I'm covered in like 900-year-old dust. I haven't told anyone, but my leg is bleeding a bit from a piece of wood scraping it when we fell. I'm not upset about the house yet, but I will be. Right now, I want them to stop telling Bax how to tie a secure knot and get me out of here.

Sam stands back and studies Bax's work. "Ever think about taking up a career in rigging?"

Bax looks confused. My sweet Bax. Josh looks at him and says, "Don't ask."

"Wasn't going to. There are things I'm happy not to know." He turns to me. "And please God let that have not been on the fuck-it list."

"It wasn't. But I do know what it is."

Josh walks around the edge of our house—no one can use

the kitchen door because of the hated bathtub. I loved it until it ruined my perfect kitchen.

He's closer to me, and David gives Sam a signal. The bed moves for a second, but David puts his hands up. We just want the ropes taut to hold the posts and frame in place. The moment the ropes steady, Josh whips me out of the bed. My ass to the wind. Whatever.

He tosses me to the corner and reaches for Bax. Bax shakes him off.

"If I move, I'm afraid the bed will fall."

"I got you." Our phones go off again. We all ignore them, of course. Mine is shattered but seems to be working. Bax takes Josh's arm and the two wrap their hands around each other's forearms. He hoists him out and off the bed just as one of the posts snaps and the bed begins slipping. Josh flings Bax at me, then the three of us watch as David signals Sam to stop. We shuffle around the edges of the house and phones are still pinging and going off. We make it outside and Sam runs in from his truck. We're watching through the door when the bed sinks about another three feet and you can only see the top of one of the posts.

"Men," I say, and they all crowd around me. I let myself be the girl and cry with relief. I'm not sure what could have gone on. But surrounded by the four men who mean the most to me is the way this should have ended. We stay like that for a moment. Baxter at my front and the rest of them in an embrace.

Our moment is broken by a loud, bossy voice in what appears to be a full wedding gown fitted around her large stomach. Stunning but still odd for one-thirty in the morning at the winery.

"WHY AREN'T YOU PEOPLE PICKING UP YOUR PHONES? And why does it look like Tabi's having a reverse harem? Where are your pants? And Bax, tuck it back. I can see the Senator." He scoots behind me quickly.

Josh breaks rank and walks towards his woman. They have three children, a girl and twin girls. Elle refuses to get married while she's pregnant and they keep getting accidentally pregnant. Fuck them.

"Assholes. I took a break from keeping my elephant ankles up in the air so listen up." She's the worst pregnant person ever, apparently even the beauty of the ballet didn't lighten her mood.

Sam grabs a pair of shorts from his truck and tosses them to Bax.

Josh pulls her to him, and she melts in his arms, she always does. He kisses her with his leftover adrenaline from hauling us out of our house. As he kisses her, the walls start to creak, and we run to Sam's truck.

Elle looks up. "What's happening?" We explain and she tsks. She's also always hated this house. She reaches into her car, pulls out leggings and tosses them to me. Thank God the woman is always prepared for all situations.

Sam asks her, "Why are you dressed as an angel?" It's seriously a beaded and sparkly dress that looks as if she can't quite zip up the back.

I yell, "Explain your angelic appearance."

Josh nods at her. "Over the years she's purchased multiple designer wedding dresses and one couture gown, and my Hellcat has proclaimed they're all useless. So, we had them altered so she could wear them. It's usually around the house. The girls think she's playing princess."

Bax lets out a sigh and says, "But you're not getting married?"

Josh stares at Elle.

She throws her hands up and says, "Oh, hell no. Not while

I'm a fucking milk making, gestating, life giving whale of a machine, and at this rate, my children will be in college before their parents get married."

Bax says, "Can we get on with this before the Seraphim sing again?"

"Fuck you. And fuck you." She hits Josh. He shrugs and she waves her arms around and does a little floaty dance, her icy blonde hair bouncing on her shoulders. "Look, consider me the Archangel Gabriel. There's a child. In the West of Oakland." She stretches her hands out and points. I just want to be anywhere else and Bax senses it. He laces our fingers together.

Josh looks confused. But David says, "We get it. You're having a baby." He smiles. Turns out he's kind of a baby guy and none of us saw that coming.

"Yes, but I'm not talking about this hellspawn who is currently kicking my kidneys and almost making me pee a little bit in my $18,000 Elie Saab."

Josh crooks an eyebrow and Elle says, "Like you don't have a billion dollars? I spent a few. Maybe when you stop knocking me up, I'll become a saver."

"You forgot to tell me." He pulls her to him.

"In my defense, I'm always fucking pregnant. My brain is fucking mush. Miserably, insufferably knocked up." Bax starts to pull me back from the crowd. I don't know where we'll go but we'll figure it out.

Elle sees us inching away. "NO! You two stay!"

Our phones pop off again.

"My phone was destroyed. Is someone dead?" I ask.

David picks up his phone. "Becca, what is it?" Sam answers his phone too.

Elle screams, "You TWO are having the baby! There's a baby in Oakland and it's yours. Becca has been trying to get a hold of you for the last couple of hours."

Bax doesn't say anything just thumb points to the falling-down house.

My body goes cold and tears spring to Bax's eyes. He moves back towards them, his voice fixed and low as if he's trying to understand aerospace equations.

Elle smiles and tears flow down her face. "They picked you. You're going to have a baby. Like tomorrow or like later on today."

David yells, "Fuck yeah," and Sam screams.

I look at Bax and sob, "But we're not ready."

"I'm ready enough for both of us. You'll be fine." Rory's words from my husband's mouth.

I blubber out a response, "Fuck. I'm going to be a mother."

And Sam says, "And Bax will be a mother fucker."

Josh smacks him, and Bax takes me in his arms. He whispers something only for me, "There is nothing in this world I love more than you. In fact, I have quite a bit overflowing. What do you say we give it to this kid who needs us? But it's your call if you're not ready." He buries his face in my neck.

"Oh, it's on. Deal."

And then the roof caves in and we run out of the way as my dream house, the one I imagined filled with kids, crumbles in on itself as Matteo and his construction crew show up.

"Well, you get your wish. You get to start from scratch. Build me a house fit enough for the Prince or Princess of Oakland."

Everyone cheers and starts to hug us, and Matteo can't seem to close his mouth as the house continues to crumble in on itself.

I continue, "And who's got a bed for us tonight?"

David winces. "We don't. Nat has a ton of volunteers staying for her big foster kid Christmas thing. They're in the

Gelbert guesthouse, Becca's pad, and there's a couple of the poor bastards shacked up with my father and mother."

I perk up because there's another solution, but then David shuts that down too. "And Sal's in town. So, Poppy's a no go." Sal Pietro is our mobster friend who is not so secretly dating David's cousin, Poppy. Sal's the head of a crime family in Los Angeles and is almost out. He's figured out how to take the entire empire legitimate, with Josh's help. His former career led them to each other, but now Josh is just a winemaker like the rest of us, except for his one investment capital client.

Bax says, "Come on. Really?" He looks to Sam who had a spare bedroom and turned it into some sex playroom thing. But I can make that work for a baby, there's a swing.

Sam shakes his head and walks over towards his truck. "Currently, no. And I have to get back, they're probably wondering where I am. Congrats on a baby not from your junk. Love you both. Glad you're not dead. Call you tomorrow."

We all groan.

Josh smiles. "We can offer you a couch or two, but the babies and nannies and my parents are at our place. Dad rented out the homestead when Mrs. Dotson skipped town with her new lover for the holidays."

Elle says, "Blessed be, we don't have to have the horrible Christmas pudding from your makeshift grandmother."

Bax looks at me. "My dad has a full house. Ingrid and Ian, and his entire family, are here for Christmas. And, Tabi, your parents are fumigating and staying at Sam's parents' house."

Elle lifts her phone and says, "MacPlace, Sonoma Inn, Three Sisters and the rest of the hotels in town are sold out."

"So, what you're telling us is there's no room at the Sonoma Mission Inn or anywhere?"

David chimes in, "Pretty much."

Bax says, "Josh and Elle's couch it is."

Josh says, "Yes, but no fucking. I've seen what your powerful lovemaking can do. And I like my floors."

〰️

I CAN'T SLEEP AND MOVE TO A DIFFERENT COUCH. BAX IS snoring. Good for him. Sleeping through my existential crisis and PTSD from falling though my house. Soreness is starting to set in, but it's not bad. The doctor said we were fine, no signs of concussion or anything wrong and that the giant bed saved us.

〰️

TABI: OUR BED FELL THROUGH OUR FLOOR TONIGHT.

RORY: And you claim my cock is too powerful? Bax must be loaded.

TABI: Yeah. Ok. Whatever. Here's the thing, there's a baby. I mean there's going to be one. And the mother chose us, but she could change her mind. And things could go horribly wrong. The little shit could turn out to not like us. Or some other fucked-up thing. And Bax and my friends are sleeping. And I have no house or a place to sleep and tomorrow I have to journey to the West to pick up a child who may or may not like me. I'm alone and thinking too much and soon I have to get up and be pleasant.

RORY: Well, that's a lie. There's no bleeding way you're going to be pleasant.

TABI: Exactly. I'm freaking out.

RORY: If it helps, so am I.

TABI: What does that even look like?

RORY: My voice gets louder.

I laugh. I know he's got a ton of joy and details to deal

with, but I can't help but lean on him when all the other men in my life have fucking disappeared into sleeping. I function better talking to men.

TABI: What if it isn't ours?

RORY: It is.

TABI: But what if?

RORY: I'm slowly bloody learning that everything is what if. You push on anyway, so you don't miss something.

TABI: Wise. Am I your best friend?

RORY: No.

TABI: Yes, I am.

RORY: Not even a little.

TABI: Oh, a little bit I am. You raging stoic wall of a kilt man.

RORY: Don't you have a child to collect?

TABI: Don't you?

RORY: {Insert Picture of baby girl asleep on his chest} I'm busy. Now bugger off.

BAX

I wake up to the jarring sight of Becca Gelbert with her legs crossed, sipping a cup of coffee, and staring at me.

"Good. You're awake."

"And you're intrusive." She's not great with social cues but a hell of a lawyer. She always seems a bit pinched and grumpy. She was born to be older, wears it like a badge. She and David were set up by genetics to be each other's foil. He's a bit more laid back.

"Be that as it may, but as of tonight you won't be able to sleep in, so get that under your hat."

I sit up and scrub my face with my hands. "Tab. Tabi, Becca needs to be official with us."

She doesn't move or open her eyes as she says, "I know, I hear her."

Becca's voice is stressed and pinched. "And you're probably going to have to be a little bit more motivated to have a baby than what I'm seeing here."

I stretch and my whole body aches like I was in a car crash. Jesus. I stand and groan.

Tabi mutters, "I feel like every part of me is angry."

Elle flutters in, in a fitted-bodice, silk, highly beaded gown with a slight train and intricate lace work on her sleeves and back. She's paired it with pink bunny slippers. Becca doesn't flinch. Not much rattles her.

I turn towards Elle and ask, "How many?"

"Well, since I was prepared to get married four different times, there are eight dresses." She places a bottle of Advil and two bottles of water on a table between Tabi and me.

Tabi says, "I won't be able to open that. I won't be able to hold things or walk or blink for like a year." I laugh and grab her four tablets and shove them in her mouth. She has the magical ability to swallow pills without water. She gulps them down, then stares at Elle. She says, "Will you marry me?"

I laugh.

"Not while I'm pregnant."

I look to Elle. "Why do you have eight dresses?"

"Ceremony and reception. And this one..." She turns in a tight circle, and it swishes like a bell. "This one kills me. It's haute couture Monique Lhuillier, it's the newest one. We were going to surprise you all and have a wedding, but you know, his super fucking sperm busted through his vasectomy to produce another life sucking demon spawn inside of me. Who I will hate with a firey passion of a thousand suns until I see its, hopefully, male, face."

"Holy shit," Becca says. I guess she can get rattled.

She's not a good pregnant person. It actually gets funnier each time.

Becca re-crosses her legs. "That's wonderful, Elle but there are more pressing issues than your attire." She looks back at us.

"I was informed of what was going on. And you should know they condemned your house this morning."

"I'm curious why my parents aren't here," Tab says. Her parents, well hell, all our parents are in way too much of our lives, and Costas and Goldie have been ready for grandkids since Tabi went to college.

"They are. I made them wait in the car," Becca replies.

Tabi rolls off the couch onto the floor and stays there, then rolls towards the door across Elle's floor. Elle laughs and Becca scoffs. I look away, her hijinks not surprising me.

Becca says, "Seriously, you're going to be a parent?"

We've all known each other way too long for that to slide.

I get in her face, and she seems surprised. "You're fucking kidding, right? She'd do anything to make you laugh. She just rolled across the floor to relieve the immense amount of pressure we're up against today. Homeless, adopting a baby and figuring the rest of it out in a matter of twenty-four hours. We never question your people skills so why the fuck are you questioning who she is? Take it back."

She says nothing. Tabi pops up on her feet and smiles at me.

I turn back to Becca, "Whatever you have to say, say it fucking fast and leave. That was your passive aggressive bully bullshit from when we were young."

Elle looks taken aback but says, "Let's not attack Tabi about her parenting skills before she's even a parent. Give her a week or so."

I stomp towards their kitchen. Tabi blows me a kiss and slips out the front door. When I reach the kitchen, Elle rubs my back until I reach for coffee.

"DRESS." I put it back and she hugs me from behind. "Let's cool down and we'll figure this out."

"How? It's Christmas Eve and we don't have a crib nor a bed."

Becca comes in the room. I glare at her.

"Don't apologize to me. Apologize to her."

Becca's holding her phone. "I will. I am sorry. Your life isn't the only one in chaos today but I shouldn't have let it affect these proceedings. I don't know where the line is sometimes. But there's something else I have to talk to you about, and it can't wait. It's just happened. Bax. Go get Tabi."

"Is it about the baby? Tell me now and I'll break it to her."

"Kind of."

Elle walks out of the room, and I panic. What if the baby is sick or the birth mom changed her mind?

Becca puts her hands out and says, "Your adoption baby is fine. He's perfect, healthy and on schedule for release this evening." I well up. Somehow knowing he's a boy makes him all the more real. A boy. Tabi will be thrilled. Becca puts her hand on my arm.

She says, "There's a wrinkle. Your adoption is closed and what I'm about to tell you won't legally change a thing. But you know how I'm your attorney for the other pursuits."

I interrupt. Tabi needs to remain calm. So whatever shit this is, I want to take the brunt of it first.

I say, "Do we have to meet the parents? Or do we just show up? And can we see a picture of the baby?"

Tabi barrels into the room. I can't stop her from hearing this. I throw my arm around her. Becca smiles and says, "I don't know what time we're supposed to show up this afternoon. They'll call us. He's perfect according to the doctor and the lawyer for the other side. It's a semi-closed situation. You'll have medical records and history, but they don't want any contact or updates. They don't want any part of his life."

I squeeze her. Then tears stream down Tabi's face. I turn her towards me. "Are you ok? We can back out," I say quickly.

"It's a boy. Thank fucking God. I would have no idea how to handle a girl."

Elle says from the living room, we knew she was listening, "Thank fucking God it's a boy. We need more boys in the next gen."

I kiss her deeply. I feel like it's the punctuation on this part of our life. As if in the next stanza the kiss will somehow be different. We're exhausted, sore and ready to be parents.

I say, "Go do your Pro/Ho stuff and deal with your parents. I'll clean up and update my dad. Then call me and we can meet up at the homestead and wait."

"Where?" She pops a hip.

I smack my forehead. "Fuck. I forgot we're homeless."

Elle walks into the kitchen in a different gown. She seriously did a costume change in the last two minutes. She takes a twirl and Tabi whistles. This one is sexy. Simple silk, deep V in the front and back. Her baby bump on display with a very visible belly button ready to pop.

She curtsies. "This was the first one. My idea of a reception dress so I could dance. But I'll never dance again. My cankles can't take it and I'm never not going to be pregnant. So, I'm in this Valentino."

We all applaud, and Josh appears holding all three little girls.

"It's gorgeous, honey. But I can't hold the succubae off any longer. The twins need to be fed and this one—" Their oldest reaches for Tabi.

"TABI!"

"Sup, little Emma. We're having a boy!" Tab raises her hand and high fives two-year old Emma. They both giggle.

"Boy! Boy! Boy!" She shrieks, then sees me and reaches for

me. She's used to being passed around and has affection for all of us. Except David's dad. But very few of us like Mr. Gelbert. Little Emma's the first of the babies to start showing up. I'm happy my son won't be too far behind her in age. My son, that phrase is blowing my mind.

Josh has a twin in each arm. I take Emma and blow raspberries into her stomach, and she giggles. Then she settles on my hip.

Josh looks. "And you doubt yourselves? You're naturals."

Tabi smacks Josh in the arm. She points at Elle. "I'm out. You work on somewhere for us to lay down our kid's sweet head. I have my parents and Pro/Ho to contend with. I literally had them drive around the block. Couldn't deal with the happy dramatic Greek sobbing. They needed to chill out."

Josh says, "I forgot we're open today. I'll try to come over and pour once I get through all my meetings this morning."

Tabi says to Josh, "Thanks. It will take my mind off things. We're not opening until eleven, and I've just decided we're having a sale. An 'I'm getting a baby, so everything is half off today' sale. And, Elle, please find me somewhere to sleep."

I squeeze Tabi as we kiss Emma yells, "There's kissing, daddy. And I want to be kissing."

Josh's voice gets deeper, "No. You're not allowed to do that until you're thirty-five." Emma turns away from him and kisses me on the cheek.

"I kiss now Daddy." Josh scowls at her. Emma's going to be so much trouble.

As she walks out the door, Elle heads to the bottom of her staircase. She looks at me. "I'm on it." There is nothing that woman can't fix, plan or maneuver, so thank God she's on our side.

I move to leave the room and Becca clears her throat.

"The wrinkle?" I forgot.

Josh gets bottles together and sticks the girls into little bouncy seats. Then scoops Emma from my arms and hands her a squeeze packet of something green and off she toddles in her diaper.

Josh claps his hands together at Becca and me. I will never get over that our brooding, titan of industry, billionaire asshole of a friend is such a girl dad.

"Becca, what's up?" Josh folds his hands over his chest and steps behind the girls to keep a watch on the bottle feeding. He adjusts one of them and nods to Becca.

"Are you sure we do this without Tabi?" Becca asks.

Josh chimes in, "That does not seem like a great idea, whatever this is."

I overrule any objections in the room. I'll hear it out and then discuss with her if she needs to know. "She has enough on her plate."

Becca's a no-nonsense gal and I'm glad for it. She blurts out, "They're yours if you still want them. Their mother surrendered them into the foster system this morning and signed away parental rights. I know all about parental rights after what went down with David, and these are iron clad. They'll scheduled to be sent to an orphanage near Chico. It's a good facility. I looked into it for you. But the state reverts to their last home to see if you want to emergency foster or follow through with adoption."

I stumble and Josh puts his hand on my back. I flip my head around the room and then land on Becca's serious face. This can't be happening. "Joaquin and Jay?"

Becca nods. "Look. I have a shit-ton of things happening right now. And now I have to be your legal team to basically get a basketball team together today. I have a ton of paperwork but I need you to decide right now. The boys are down south of San Jose in a random DCF office. They don't know about you and Tabi getting to decide. But it is your choice."

Our foster boys were only with us for five months when their mother wanted them back. That hurt more than the miscarriages. Tabi never quite bounced back. She's still Tabi and still perfect, but there's a dull spot on her heart where those boys should be.

My voice breaks. How much more can this day be? "There isn't a choice. Today we become a family of five."

"From none, to outnumbered. Are you sure?" Josh puts his hand on my shoulder, and I cover it and squeeze. I'm sure.

I smile and again tears spring to my eyes. "So, fucking sure. And I do not need to consult Tabi. Do it. I'll go down and get the boys right now and we'll surprise her at the hospital in Oakland."

Elle enters, a weepy mess. Josh disregards it and mutters. "Hormones."

"Those boys. I love them. I'm so happy." Elle breaks into a sob.

"Not only do we love them, and they're supposed to be ours, but knowing Natalie and her story, there's no fucking way we're not doing this." David's wife was a foster kid who was never adopted.

"You're still homeless," Becca says.

Shit. "Elle, find me a VBRO, anything. A tent. Find me beds, a crib, a bale of hay. Anything. And no one tell anyone about this. Oh shit. Christmas."

"Get your siblings and friends on the Christmas thing," Becca offers up.

Josh says, "Sam and David are out with the woolly weeders today, in the back vineyards of Pro/Ho."

"Becca, do you need to be with me to pick the boys up?"

"I'm not sure but someone legally has to be with Tabi. They hand me the baby then you. Let me figure it out."

I clap and begin to pace around their living room. Everyone joins me out there. A plan is coming together. My head flips from the emotion of the moment to taking care of shit. Natalie was my assistant for years and details are her thing. "Nat can keep all of this straight, Elle, get her to help you. Becca, tell them I'm coming to our kids. I'm showering and changing into Josh's clothes. Then I'm headed to San Jose. I'll meet you in Oakland at what time?"

"I think around four or five, they can't be specific. Once the hospital releases the birth mother, they can release the baby to you." I nod.

Josh says, "What do I do?"

"We're all going to Gelbert's winery tonight for Christmas eve, right?" I say, and he nods. "RSVP for five for us. And help Tab at Pro/Ho. Tell Poppy we need a Christmas dinner and stock whatever fucking fridge we happen to have with food. And nobody tell Tabi." Poppy Gelbert's a chef, and I'll need to feed these kids once we are wherever the hell we're going. I add one more thing, "Try to keep it from Sam as well." Sam is shit with secrets. I walk upstairs and call my dad.

"Son!"

"Hey, are you sure there's not a spare cot or something for Tabi and me?"

"And the baby. Oh, don't you forget that baby, son. I'm itching for it. We could figure something out, maybe. But there's a lot of them in that family."

I laugh at him. He has a full house of Ingrid's boyfriend's family. He has one other grandkid but turns out my dad is a born grandpa. My mother would have loved this moment of chaos that's all resulting from an abundance of love. It's not often I get caught up in wishing she were still alive, but today, it would be nice.

I answer my father, "I know but with the house down, I just don't want to shove the baby in a closet. Elle's working on it."

"Then you're golden, son. She'll figure it out. Call me if there's something I can do. I'm trying to stay out of the way because I figure, Goldie is all up in it."

"My mother-in-law is certainly enthusiastic but don't take a back seat to her, dad. Hey, if you have a moment to take over for Tab pouring at Pro/ho that would be a huge help."

"Consider it done. I'll get over there when I can. Love you, Bax."

"You too. Thanks, Dad."

I hang up and dial my youngest sister.

I speak before she does, "Ingrid!"

"It's Ian. What's up, man? She's in the shower."

"Do you make a habit of picking up your girlfriend's phone?" I like this guy, but I'm still wary that he's a little older, an international rockstar with a billion number one hits and one very public nasty divorce.

"Yes. I'm that possessive and controlling. She's not allowed to talk to anyone unless I approve. Be afraid of me, Bax." He pauses then says, "She told me to answer if it was you or Tabi. After everything that's happened in the last twelve hours, she thought she might be needed. Hold on, I'm supposed to give her the phone in the shower."

"Not enjoying the idea of you seeing my sister naked."

"I'll avert my eyes."

"Good."

I wait through the giggles and what sounds like an ass slap, and hum. "Bax, what's up?"

"Keep this close. Tabi doesn't even know I'm about to give her the ultimate Christmas present."

"Tell me it's better than that piece of shit house you gave her when you got married."

"Joaquin and Jay."

"OH MY GOD. OH MY GOD. I'm going to be an auntie like three times over TODAY. You're the best, Bax!"

"Glad you're thrilled, but I need presents. Boy presents. Ten and eight-year-old presents. I'm tapping David to get Jay art supplies, but Joaquin plays a little guitar. We were somewhere once and he plucked out a song on an old guitar that he remembered, and he lit up. Get him all the stuff. And sports stuff. They love soccer. Shit, I should have David do that too. And Harry Potter. Get them Ravenclaw and Gryffindor stuff. And the whole set of books. Get the illustrated ones and the regular ones. And all the merch. We'll teach them to be more tolerant than JK, but she wrote a hell of a series."

"Which is which?'

"Shit. Um Jay. Jay is the Ravenclaw."

"Got it. Go get those fabulous boys. I love you, Bax. You're truly the best. Tabi's going to fucking flip. And you're going to be the absolute best dad. I'm weepy!"

"Love you, Ingrid."

"Do they still believe?"

"I don't know if they do, but I certainly do."

A tingle of excitement runs down my spine as I say this.

15

TABI

Goldie is a mess. She's driving me crazy and Yia Yia's in the back of the car. She's like 120 years old. We have no idea. Her skin is so leathery it's hard to actually tell her age. For all I know she could be sixty and my mother's sister instead of her mom. I lean into the car.

"Tabitha, we have much to do for the babe." I roll my eyes and she admonishes me. "That is no way to be a mother."

"Pretty sure I'm not going to be the mother you expect."

My father's voice booms from the driver's seat as he chuckles, "You will be exactly what we expect."

Yia Yia puts her hands up in celebration. She's wearing a yellow slicker. It's not raining. When her arms go up, I notice she's not wearing anything else.

"Where are Yia Yia's pants?"

My mother claps her hands. "Who has time for pants when there is a baby coming. And soon. The baby that will be my

157

grandbaby. The one who will need things. Yia Yia is fine in her slicker coat. The baby needs gifts, now."

And that is how I will get my parents out of my hair today.

I gesture to them. "Then by all means go and get them. The three of you go get all the gifts the baby will need. I give you my blessing. Hail Mary, full of grace the lord is with thee."

My father smiles and says, "Blessed are the fruits of thy womb."

My mother looks at him and does her anti-curse hiss. "Tut, tut, tut." Then she spits on the ground. "Her womb is not where this baby is coming from. Do not curse her womb further."

This ethnic road show needs to pull out. "You can't go shopping with Yia Yia like that."

"The slicker coat covers her fine. We'll buy her pants at the T.J. Maxx." Goldie loves a bargain.

"Go and get all the gifts. I don't know what the fuck Frank-incense is but go get some of that too. It can't hurt." My mother shrieks she's so excited, hopefully this should keep her busy. Yia Yia is dancing in the backseat. "Have fun, kids. And don't forget to cover up Yia Yia's leathery cooch before I lose my breakfast. I'm headed to work."

My mother smacks my arm, "But you have a baby coming."

"And a winery to run. And a house to uncondemn and parents who need to go buy the baby boy some things." I shift my legs. I'm so uncomfortable and fucking sore from the after-math of falling through a floor and some rough sex. Sex. Are we ever having that again? I hear a newborn can cramp that little habit.

My father's voice pulls me back to reality, he chuffs, "JES!" Then he makes a fist and pulls it back. He was raised in a family of brothers and—even though now I know I'm not a disappointment to him at all—he loves boys.

Yia Yia runs from the car as everyone is buckling in and sprints across Elle and Josh's lawn. Their house is way up on a hill with a private drive coming up from their winery. Not sure where she's going but she found a plastic crown.

I start scream singing her walk out song. Yes, she has one, and it was the mistake of my life giving it to her. She won't go anywhere without it. But she does respond instantly by dancing. She thinks they're saying "Yia Yia" instead of "Yeah Yeah." I use it to my advantage. "Take that, rewind it back..." And she freezes. Then she saunters back to me as I roll through all the lyrics. By the time she arrives she's rapping the Ludacris part. I sing along to the line, 'freak in the bed'. Then we strap her into the car with the crown firmly on her head.

My father yells as they pull down the driveway, "We'll go to the shopping. Then you meet us with the baby."

☙❧

I INCH OPEN THE DOOR TO PRO/HO'S TASTING ROOM. IT used to be a long shed, but we built it out. There's a bar that David created, made of all the license plates we pulled from the grounds as we built out our winery. His sculptures are kind of awesome. He has a red blend releasing in the spring with a replica of our bar on its label. He's calling the wine "Side Hustle."

I flip on all the Christmas lights and prep for visitors. I glance out the window and see the remains of my house. I pull out my phone while I work. I play my favorite new Christmas album. They all hate it, but I LOVE Leslie Odom Jr. I'm the only one who roots for Burr when we watch Hamilton.

My phone rings and unless it's Becca, Bax or Elle, I'm not biting today. It's the hospital with a follow-up or a billing question, I'm sure. It can wait, I need to update some people on my current sitch.

TABI: Who's up for some shocking fucking news?

BEN: Happy Christmas, everyone.

TABI: That's all well and fine, Ben, but I have actual news.

RORY: Bit busy but what?

SABRINA: Hit me. I'm drunk at my sister's house and Patrick keeps not so subtly hinting that he loves me the most. But how deep is his love?

JONATHAN: Is that weepy four-drink Sabrina who quotes the Bee Gees?

SABRINA: Not weepy. I'm happy. Let's say it's six-drink Sabrina. Who thinks there may be a move-in question coming? Who's all a titter with excitement?

TRISTAN: Has anyone ever died from southern fruitcake? And what pray to the saints above is biscuit gravy?

TABI: Focus. I'M GETTING A BABY.

RORY: Been there, done that.

JONATHAN: Holy shit, was that a joke, Rory? Did you tell a joke?

TABI: Stay in your lane, Scotch Egg.

RORY: Fair enough. There's someone more important than you, Tab, that I have to handle. Update me later.

SABRINA: WHEN? This is exciting, isn't it?

TRISTAN: Why do you keep ending every text with a dumb question? Like you're 80 years old?

SABRINA: Six-drink Sabrina likes question marks. But does it matter in the scheme of things?

JONATHAN: You did it again. You're six-drink Sabrina has morphed into six-drink Grandma Sabrina.

BEN: That's wonderful! I was going to tell you I got a ring for Laurie, but Tabi beat me out. That's so fantastic.

TABI: Did I mention I'm getting a baby? Did anyone hear that?

BEN: I did.

TABI: Thank you, Ben

JONATHAN: Not from your junk?

TABI: Nah, some little boy whose parents decided we were the better choice.

TABI: Rory?

TABI: Come on, I totally set you up, Kilt.

TRISTAN: Mate, she teed that up pretty well. It's an easy take down.

TABI: Must be changing a diaper.

SABRINA: I'll do it. Better choice? Was there no one else?

JONATHAN: Better choice? Did you put your fuck-it list in your application?

BEN: Better choice? Are they out of parents in California?

TABI: Solid burns all around.

TRISTAN: Better choice? For what? Teaching the lad how to drink and insert himself into other's lives without asking?

TABI: Again, solid.

RORY: There's no better choice.

TABI: Softie.

RORY: Not often, ask Zoe.

I laugh and lean over the bar to reach something, and my tits ache. And he didn't have sex with them last night. I could attribute it to falling two floors, but they hurt yesterday too. And my back is a touch sore. I stopped keeping track of my period when we went off the shots. And I was warned my system would be screwed up for a minute.

Oh. Shit. Wait. Fuck me. I have so much to do, and this is now very curious. I'm not sure when I had my last period. This can't be possible. I fell through a floor. Shit. I have twenty minutes until I'm open. I dash out of the tasting room. I bolt inside Walgreens screaming, "Where's the bathroom?"

৩৯৯

THAT'S AN INTERESTING FUCKING DEVELOPMENT. I'M BACK in the tasting room. No one is here. No cars are pulling in. Might be all the trucks pulling debris off my house keeping them away. I can't just sit here. I'm not sure what to do. Or if it's even real. Four sticks say it's real, but they could be lying muthafuckers. Is it possible we'll have two kids under the age of one? All in one day. That's a twisted little turn of fate. I don't know how to stop my head from reeling.

I check my messages, the doctor I ignored. The hospital calls. Shit. I listen to my messages and it's the doc, he needs to talk to me. He knows. He knows about the sticks. I had to pee in a cup last night. What if I fucked up the kid before it's a kid when my bed went sailing through the floor? Oh shit. Rough sex. Can a baby handle that? I mean, he slammed me pretty good last night. Can he reach the baby? Will the baby be pissed off being poked in the head? It doesn't have a head yet, does it? I spent so much time trying to get pregnant I forgot to research how to actually be pregnant. Or a parent for that matter.

My phone pings. I shoot off a text so I'm not ignoring them.

SABRINA: Tab- you there? Who is this darling baby joining our ranks?

BEN: You really are grandmaesque right now, Bree.

TABI: I'm back. Sorry. Yes, Jonathan, not from my junk. There's a little boy in Oakland who's going to be ours tonight. Merry Christmas. You bitches were the best part of my year. Aside from the foster boys. But you certainly were the most fun.

TRISTAN: That's awfully sweet of you. Maternal instinct kicking in?

TABI: Fuck off.

BEN: Your baby is right on time. If you actually did get pregnant then you wouldn't be there for this child.

JONATHAN: That sounds like something I would have said. But I agree with Ben. If this year taught me nothing else, it's that timing is everything. It's all as it should be.

Yeah, cool. So pregnant and a newborn all in the last day. Bax will laugh his head off or sob. I walk out in the back of the tasting room, lean over the garbage can and puke. Not because I have morning sickness, just because this is a lot to handle on an empty stomach. Should I call Bax? Do I tell him now? No, I'm going to tell him when I see him. I'll tell him while we pick up our other child. Our other child. This is blowing my mind. I need to make sure the baby is ok before I tell him. What if it's not really ok.

And there's no way I'm giving him this Christmas present over the phone. That's bullshit. I want the full reaction. We've waited too long.

I will fucking rule Christmas. The best present ever.

"This is Tabitha Aganos."

The nurse screams, "It's her! Yes, my dear! We're waiting for you."

"I need to confirm a something."

"We know! Come in right now so we can confirm the heartbeat!"

I know this well-meaning bitch is excited, but that sentence terrifies me. Confirm a heartbeat, like there's a good chance there won't be one. Sadly, I'm more familiar with that part. I wish Bax were here, but if there's something wrong, at least I can keep that from him. I'll tell him in a couple of days when we're exhausted and happy newborn parents. It won't sting as much for him. Either way it's my Christmas present to him.

She squeals loudly. "Come. Now!"

I hang our closed sign and squeal out of our parking lot again.

I TURN THE CORNER ONTO OUR BACK VINEYARD PROPERTY and drive through the path as much as I can. I park and stand on the front of my car. Finally, I spot the flock. There are a large number of sheep spread through the vines eating our weeds and brush. Instead of spraying or pulling we have the sheep come out and help keep things biodynamic and organic. We're not totally either yet, but it's the goal. But those woolly little fuckers do an excellent job. They can eat noxious plants and help keep the brush under control for fire damage. I head in the direction of the animals and the ones tending to them.

"Yo. Shepherds!" Both of them look to me, then cover their eyes.

Sam yells, "Tab."

But David yells, "Yo. Mary. Think maybe you can turn off the multitude of heavenly host?" I realize my car lights are on bright and pointed directly at them. I click my car into park and the lights go out.

"Ha ha, funnier than you know. I need one of you to go and run the tasting room. I can't find anyone else, and I have to go. Josh and Adrian Schroeder said he'd help later."

Sam folds his arms and David takes a stance that says they're not going to do shit. This is their favorite. It's my favorite too, just being out here in the vines. With the quiet. It's the only time my head settles or feels even remotely normal. I know they feel the same. And they love being with the sheep. The owners of the flock actually trust them enough to take a break. They drop them off and come back for them. Sam's dogs are running everywhere, and the sheep ignore them.

My phone dings a text.

Sonoma Medical: Your appointment began five minutes ago. Please call the desk if cancelling.

I point to Sam. He shakes his head no. This is the new asshole Sam.

"Don't make me take you to task there late blooming player. You. Get your ass in gear and get to the tasting room."

He turns away. I don't want to tell them but he's pissing me off.

"Do it," I yell.

David chuckles. "I'll do it," he says and begins to walk.

Sam stops him and yells at me, "No. You get your ass back there. You signed up for this shift and we're all fucking busy. We're going to have to pick up your slack soon enough. Handle it."

That's not Sam. His pain has morphed into assholery. "Damn, I hope the real Sam comes home for Christmas. Are you hungry, muthafucker? Is that what's making you so cranky? I have something I can't miss."

David flips Sam off and joins me.

Sam yells, "You have a thing later, Bee. The baby is later. Right now, you have nothing."

I round on him and let loose again. Fuck it. My hand reflexively goes to my stomach. "Or I have a fucking ultrasound to make sure that there's a heartbeat, so I can be twice a mother today. Blessed be, asshole." I catch a glimpse of Sam's face turn pale as I turn and run back to the car. I did not want to do that. I wanted to keep it for just Bax. "And don't fucking tell a fucking soul, you asshole, piece-of-shit, lousy secret keeper. If you do one cocksucking thing right today that's not being a prick, do that."

I'm almost to the car, David quick on my heels. He catches

me easily and flips me towards him. His strong arms pull me to him, and he kisses the top of my head and squeezes me tight.

My voice wobbles, "What if there isn't one?"

His voice is low and strong, "There will be."

"What if it's not true? What if I miscarry again?"

"It is and you won't. And if there isn't and you don't, who fucking cares. You're Tabi Aganos, you're afraid of nothing."

"How do you know?"

"Because this is super fucked up that you finally get a kid to adopt and now, you're pregnant. It's too insane to not be true. It's just too Tabi. All or nothing." He squeezes me closer, and I stop myself from crying. Sam is about a foot away when I break from David.

He looks down at his feet and rubs his chin where his beard used to be. His voice is low. His hand is on my back then he pulls me to him. "We got all this, my sister. I'm sorry. I'm not sure who I'm supposed to be lately."

I squeeze him tighter and he kisses the top of my head.

"Don't tell Bax!" Sam's the worst fucking secret keeper. I'm an idiot to tell him. "In fact, stay away from him. And all people today."

"I got you, Tab. I'm also a little afraid of hormonal Tabi, so I promise to avoid Bax. Love you, Bee."

I'm at a red light and I can't help myself.

TABI: I might be knocked up.

RORY: In addition to the other kid.

TABI: Yes.

RORY: Why are you so extra? Americans—do you do anything small and quiet?

TABI: I don't.

RORY: This I know.

TABI: I'm on my way to confirm it all.

RORY: Then by all means please keep texting me. Drive, you daft woman. Drive. We need answers.

I toss my phone and speed like hell to get to my appointment, grateful my friends and the grump across the pond are all pulling for me. It can't hurt to have more people putting positive vibes into this.

❧ 16 ❧

BAX

I pull up to the tasting room to see if she's still there and I'm greeted by David throwing a party. It's packed and he's running it like a pro. Run-DMC is blaring, and everyone is rapping along with the lyrics. My father's here, dancing. He doesn't usually do that, but he's pouring while David stands on a stool behind the bar dancing.

I step behind the bar and several people say, "Hello, Mr. Mayor." I grin and nod. I pour a couple of tastes, then look at David.

"Where's Tab?"

He cracks his knuckles. His tell. No matter what comes out of his mouth, it's a lie. "She had to take care of stuff for the baby."

Sam enters, sees me and turns right around. He'll crack. I turn to chase him down, and David pulls me back.

David says casually as he rings up a customer, "Can you help us out here?"

"Can you tell me the truth?" I shoot back.

"No. I can't, but please don't ask Sam." He smirks and raises his eyebrows at me.

"Fine. If you can keep her secret, you can keep mine." I grin and pour some more. David leans down and grabs another bottle and opens it while staring at me.

"Joaquin and Jay are coming home today. I'm heading south of San Jose to get them in a minute. But I want it to be a surprise for Tab. I'm bringing the boys to the hospital to meet their new brother."

My father hoots, I assume Ingrid told him. He hugs me.

"So fucking pleased at all of this, my boy." He grins then goes back to shaking his ass for the patrons. I laugh hard at the overexcited grandpa.

David's eyes are crazy wide, and the bottle he's holding is slipping from his hand. I don't catch it in time, and it shatters. Everyone in here, as well as myself, yells, "OPA!" It's written on a sign behind us. She wanted everyone to know smashing plates, in our case bottles or glasses, signals the end and the beginning, to ward off evil spirits and to express abundance. It's eerily apt today.

David isn't moving as I begin to pick up the pieces. It's like he's frozen.

"I know, it's shocking."

He cocks an eyebrow and smirks at me. "It certainly is. It certainly fucking is." He lifts me into a giant bear hug.

"Thanks, man."

"You're never sleeping again." He grins. "Wow. That is an abundance of riches you two got going." I grin as David continues talking while we both clean up and keep pouring. Working side by side quickly to get everyone happy. "That's some full house you got. Oh, wait. You don't have a house." He's laughing. Hard. "And you have so many, many children all of a sudden." He's bent over and can't speak. It's not that bad. Is it? I don't have time to think about it. I have to go.

"I need a favor."

"Apparently, I'm your family's go to guy today. By the by, Nat's going to sob at your feet, you know?"

"I do. And this is partially her fault." Nat's the one who encouraged us to foster older kids instead of babies. Second best decision of my life. Taking Tabi's hand when I was five was the first.

David rolls his wrists towards himself. "Hit me up. What else can we do for the new Schroeder clan today?"

"We?"

"You don't think I can hold all these secrets, do you? I gotta tell Natalie."

"I need boy presents for tomorrow. Art and sports. Ingrid is handling music and some other stuff."

My dad yells to me, "GO! And turn up the volume on this joyous day!" I kiss my dad's cheek and race out of the tasting room to the car and look down at my pants. I have wine splashed up on them. Whatever. I stare at our house being ripped apart by Matteo and his machines and wonder if he can salvage some pants. I dump a bottle of water on the stain and pat dry with a workout shirt in the back of my car.

I hear David yell from inside, "Ok. Everybody grab two bottles on the house and get the hell out. Merry Christmas from Pro/Ho and the baby Jesus, who is apparently on his way here with a whole troupe of newly minted apostles. Get out!"

I grin and vow to pay for all those bottles to fix our books.

TABI: I'm a wreck. Tell me you have diapers and shit I can use until I can order a bunch of shit from the comfort of someone's couch.

DAVID: Yes. And what we don't have Elle will. But you should know, you're going to have to actually take care of it.

TABI: Them.

DAVID: Healthy.

TABI: Both of us. And apparently rough sex is totally fine.

DAVID: Good to know. Seriously. Sure, you're, ok?

TABI: We're quite fine. I'm fucking stunned, but the tiny thing is healthy and strong. And big. I haven't been paying attention longer than I knew.

DAVID: How many?

TABI: Four months. I just thought I'd been eating and drinking too much.

DAVID: Drinking. Shit.

TABI: They're not worried but I mean, what else should we be feeding one of our kids?

DAVID: True dat. Should get Nat on a regime of Merlot and Chardonnay.

TABI: Really?

DAVID: Everything's coming up babies.

TABI: You sly ginger bastard.

I'M BACK AT JOSH'S HOUSE AND NO ONE IS HERE. I'M TRYING to find clothes that aren't too fancy. Elle doesn't do casual often, and I certainly don't want to put on one of the wedding dresses. Her closet is big enough for my family. Oh. My. GOD. My family. My phone rings, and it's my dad. I'm sorting through her jeans, and I answer.

"I'm at Elle and Josh's house."

"We are on our way to show you the things."

"Nope, show each other, no time for the wacky Greeks bearing gifts right now." I have to hustle back to Pro/Ho.

I peel off my leggings and pull on her jeans that have elastic. I grab a navy blouse that seems to be ironed and perfect and look at myself. I don't look like a mother. I hold what I thought was cheese bloat and realize it's a baby. My belly is more godlike than gouda.

I'm slightly rounded. Elle and I are pregnant together. This kid will have instant family, a crap ton of cousins and a sibling. I hope it's a boy. I demanded they tell me, and they kept insisting it was too early to tell. I think they're liars.

"Kid. Do me a favor. Stick around and meet us, ok. It's going to be a touch chaotic, but I promise you a hell of a ride." I put my other hand over my stomach and shake off sentiment. Today is a joyous disaster so far. My father's voice, downstairs, brings me back.

Costas says, "There's still a baby, right?" I freeze. Which baby? Oh. The other baby, not this one that I'm hauling around. I run downstairs and he's got his brow furrowed and it appears he's alone.

I say, "Theoretically. I can't find Bax."

"Your mother wanted you to know that you should and could stay at the fancy Sonoma Mission Inn. That place is very large, and we will pay."

They don't spend money like that, and it's a sweet gesture. But I already tried all the hotels in town. We could go to a hotel away from town up in Santa Rosa, or find someplace in San Francisco, but I kind of want to be near our insane family.

"Efcharistó kalí mou katsíka tou patéra. Alas, there's no room at the Sonoma Mission Inn. Or any inn or Best Western. I'm fucking Mary with a virgin birth and nowhere to put this kid to sleep."

"You stay in the bed we are sleeping in at Langerfords."

They're at Sam's parent's house for the holidays while theirs gets fumigated. Yia Yia may have a food hoarding issue and treats her closet like a pantry. The canned goods are fine, but the old watermelon and pita are not.

He straightens his shoulders as if he's making an emphatic statement. "Your mother and I will sleep in the camper."

I toss my keys in my purse and turn back towards him, "What FUCKING CAMPER?"

"Don't you swear at me. The camper that I've always dreamed of buying."

I put my hands on his shoulders, "Do not buy an RV because our piece-of-shit dream house imploded. We'll figure this out. I'll call you later after I have the kid. Take the women and go have a fabulous lunch. Or go buy more stuff for your grandbaby." His eyes flood, he really is a silly goat. "I love you, Baba. But I'm serious, go away, Dad. I do not have time for the Greeks today."

My father nods sharply once and kisses me on the forehead then leaves. I wave to my mother who is still crying from happiness and toss a hunk of cheese down my throat. Who cares about the cheese bloat now? I don't even slice it. I just eat this Vella Dry Jack cheese like it's an apple. David hasn't called so I have no idea what the fuck is going on over there.

I answer my phone while chewing and without pretense, Becca utters, "Tabitha, we need for you to go to the hospital right now."

"Now. Now. Bax isn't answering his phone. Baxter. I have to find Bax. This is too soon." Becca's not only our lawyer, but our court-appointed case worker. Becca got certified so we wouldn't have to deal with a stranger if this all ever came up. Her tone shifts when I don't say anything else.

"Wake up, Tabi!!! TABI! This is it. Baxter is dealing with another legal issue for the city. He'll join you there as soon as possible, but we have to go get your baby! Be ready to leave in ten minutes."

"I'm at Elle and Josh's."

Becca Gelbert is never this excited; she's the opposite of her brother. Even though they're both gorgeous, ginger and tall, that's where the similarities end. She's the most reserved of us all. In fact, she's usually the grumpiest of us all.

I hold my stomach, breathe in sharply and call Bax. He doesn't answer.

"MUTHAFUCKER. Call me. Call me. We have to head to Oakland now. The baby is ready. Is that a thing? Like takeout? Ma'am, your baby's ready for pick up. Call me. Please. I love you. Let's go meet our kid." I text while throwing up the cheese. I'm out of the first trimester so I shouldn't be throwing up like this, but I'm so nervous.

TABI: You have to stop the city shit. You have to come to Josh and Elle's NOW. Becca is picking us up in like ten minutes.

I start running around the room fixing pillows and arranging things on the tables. Elle will be pissed. She likes things very particular, but I need something to do. I wish someone were here. I'm a wreck and Becca's not really the emotional support I need.

TABI: Hey. Anyone. I'm freaking out. It's time. It's time to go get the baby. And other things have happened. And I don't know where I'm sleeping, and I realize now this is probably the most vulnerable I've been with you people.

SABRINA: What can I do? Do you want to be snarky to me? Will that help?

TABI: A little.

SABRINA: Patrick just asked me to move in with him. I'm thinking about it.

TABI: Really? You're in love with him and that city is fucking expensive. If you don't move in with him for lust and fucking, at least do it for the real estate.

SABRINA: *Feel better?*

TABI: *A little.*

SABRINA: *Good. I said yes, just wanted to give you something to snark about.*

BEN: *I'm thinking of getting a mullet haircut.*

TABI: *You go achy breaky. Let your redneck freak flag fly.*

JONATHAN: *We're renaming the farm Paradise City.*

TABI: *Where the grass is green, and the girls are pretty? That's the dumbest fucking idea I've ever heard. Do you know you're only going to attract metal heads and nudists?*

TRISTAN: *Sherilyn and I have decided to finance Axle's new business. He's venturing into crypto coin—he's calling it, Axle's Serious Scratch.*

TABI: *He's calling it A.S.S.? Cuz that's a sound investment. Seems like a solid future for the two of you. I'm sure you'll be happy while you're poor. At least you'll have a souped-up airbrushed piece-of-shit art car to live in.*

RORY: *I'm breathing.*

TABI: *And that's quite enough out of you, Highland Fling. Tuck your caber under your kilt and shut the hell up.*

RORY: *Now pull your Mama bear britches up and go get your kid.*

I smile and head to the front door. They get me.

Becca is ten minutes late and I'm starting to freak out because there isn't really a kid on the other end of this and it's all an elaborate prank. I'm sitting on the front steps and waiting having left messages for everyone, and no one is around. I sent my parents away and now when I could possibly use them, they're not picking up. I text Bax the address of the hospital and plead with him to meet me as soon as possible. I can't believe he's missing this.

I check my phone again, then I hear a cheery voice laughing. My head jerks to the right following the voice.

"What the fuck are you doing here, Poppy?" She's a chef with a small café on the edge of the center square in downtown Sonoma, and David and Becca's cousin. She's like a little sister, but she's a rule-following good girl. So, we've had our issues. But she's also not-so-secretly dating a mafia don. She's got range.

"Is that anyway to speak to me?" She pulls a headband from her pocket and smooths back her red curls. She has hair a lot like Rory's Zoe, at least from what I can tell from the pictures of the new mama.

She stands her ground, "I'm here to hold your hand." I grin at the phrase and as I approach her, she throws herself at me. We hug and I hold on a little longer than she does. "Hmm. Seems somebody was intuitive enough to know you'd need me."

"I'll be fine if I can find Bax." I bat back some tears from my eyes and shake it off. Fuck this wheel of gouda sized thing in my belly is making me weepy.

"He'll be there and so will Becca. But in the meantime, I've been deputized by the state of California so I can escort you to the hospital and hold that baby in case Bec doesn't get there in time. Let's go!"

I look around and there's a giant grey Volvo SUV parked on the side of the house. Poppy has a Tesla. "Whose car?"

She hands me the keys. "Yours."

"What are you talking about?" I run to the car. It's gorgeous. I'm seriously freaking out that Bax bought us a family car.

Poppy smiles and says reading off her phone, "I'm supposed to tell you it's not a true Donk, but it should do the trick getting where you need to be."

When I was little, my dream was to own a car with the nickname Donk, a classic 1972 Chevy Impala, because I thought it looked bad ass and loved the name. I've told lots of people about that, but I've only told one person in the last ten years.

I spin around. Her grin gets even wider. "It's a baby gift."

Poppy skips over to the car and opens the back door. There's a car seat already installed and stacks of diapers in the back. My eyes fill with tears because this is so kind.

She hands me a card that simply says:

They say beware of Greeks bearing gifts, but nothing about Italians. Congrats bravo bambino selvaggio.

S.

He calls me 'wild child little sister'. I turn to Poppy and she's bouncing on her toes. "He bought it, it's all legal." It has to be since he's been working with the FBI on taking down other illegal factions in his line of work. While he goes legit, he's crumbling the gang network in LA. He's a good mobster if there is such a thing.

I say, "Your boyfriend bought me a car."

"He's not my boyfriend, just a friend."

I start laughing. "Bull-fucking-shit. But I'll happily accept the maestro of the mafia's big fat fucking present." I take a picture of it and send it to Bax.

TABI: I don't know what the fuck meeting you're in but the city better be burning down. Sal gave us a car. You gave me nothing today. Except a quick grope in the downstairs bathroom, which I'm grateful for, but still. It's not a Volvo.

BAX: Sorry. Busy. Love you.

TABI: You know I'm getting in this car, which we're calling Donk, to go retrieve your child and this is the first you're contacting me.

BAX: I know. I'm so sorry. I'm in serious urgent business. I love you. I'll meet you there. And that grope wasn't long enough but I'll makes sure to Volvo grope you soon. You know when we ever get sleep or have a moment or even a pillow.

BAX: GTG. I promise this is all worth it. There is nothing in this world or the next that will ever be as important to me as you and what we're doing today, Bee.

TABI: Fuck you for trying to make me cry. I don't have time for that shit. I love you too. Maybe not as poetic or as much as you love me, but it's a lot.

I turn the phone to Poppy and shrug. "Ok, you're up."

Poppy teases me, "Admit it."

I roll my eyes. "I need you to be my emotional support, happy?"

Poppy squeals and hugs me again. "Yes. Very."

"Let's go get my baby and hopefully his father will show up at some point." This isn't like the most reliable human on the planet. He'll figure it out. But fuck, whatever is happening must be important. He chose me over everything in the past so whatever this is must be insanely complicated. But I don't like it. I don't like being in the dark like this, especially today. I have to shake off this feeling of dread that's creeping up. Squash it like a rotten grape.

I grab her phone.

"HEY!" she yells.

I shove it in front of her face for recognition, then pull her towards me and pop off a selfie of us and the car. I assume she has his newest number. The rest of us have to flail through a system of burner phones to get to him. Ain't nobody got time for that today. I text him from her phone.

POPPY (TABI): You crafty muthafucking godfather.

SAL: Am I now? Will there be a ceremony or some shit?

POPPY (TABI): Nah, he's got way too many people in his life to take on a real godfather. Thank you. Here's a picture of a pretty good moment.

SAL: *The car you keep, the girl not so much. Now go. Tell Ginger-snap to call me later and be nice. Have her send me a picture when you crumble and cry like a little bitch.*

POPPY (TABI): *Never.*

SAL: *Cent'Anni (hundred years)*

POPPY (TABI): *Cent'Anni*

"Let's go, deputy Poppy. It's time to saddle up and ride."

She hops in the passenger seat, and I buckle up.

I freeze and Poppy turns to me. "You, ok?"

I unbuckle. My hands are shaking like a leaf. "Can you drive?"

She just grips my hand and holds tight.

❧ 17 ❧

BAX

Traffic is, of course, not on my side. Ingrid and David got all the shopping and wrapping done and are taking the presents to wherever the hell we're sleeping tonight. I know we'll probably end up in Santa Rosa or Napa at a Hampton Inn or something. Anything will be fine because we'll be together. Shit. We need at least two beds.

I'm sitting about twenty minutes from San Jose. And have been for about an hour now. Fuck me, I have to be in Oakland, like now. There's no way. This has turned into a shitshow.

"Siri, call Elle."

"What's up, Big Poppa!"

"Don't call me that."

"Gonna keep doing it."

"I need more beds." I grip the steering wheel as I say it. I can't even wrap my head around all of this. "Holy shit! Elle. We need more beds. Like solid real beds for boys."

She says, "I know."

"Of course, you do. I just wanted to make it clear that whatever you're putting together included all of us."

"Calm down. But shouldn't you be in Oakland? It's happening now. Do you know that?"

"Yes, but I'm still stuck in traffic, and I don't have the boys and Tabi will never forgive me for missing this."

"And that's what makes you Big Poppa. It's often a choice between two things that you feel might be letting someone down. Welcome to parenthood."

"It's good though, right?"

"The best. Pregnancy is the fucking worst. But you don't have to do that."

"I'm freaking the fuck out. I am going to have three children by the end of the day. And Tabi's going to kill me for not being with her because California traffic is going to cause me to miss it all. I'm honest to God going to end up divorced and be a weekend dad because of fucking urban planning and the ever-expanding population of the Bear Flag state."

"Breathe."

"WE can't do that here." The car inches forward and I bang on the wheel. "Because the air quality is shit. We have enough money and no more room. Go to Oklahoma people! Stop coming to California! STOP. We're full!"

I'm spinning out of control, and the only person who ever grounds me or who can stop this spiral is the one person I can't talk to right now because she's spinning out as well. Good lord, I'm codependent.

"We got you. We all do. Go get the newest members of our tribe, no matter how long it takes. They need you, and you're doing the right thing. Tabi will understand. She won't be angry at the end of the day."

There's silence on the phone and I relax a touch as the car moves forward.

"Elle, I don't want to bring the boys back to a hotel. Can we move some shit around with my dad? Get the future maybe-in-laws to leave? What's happening at your guest house?"

"Rented. And it's Christmas, Bax. We can't kick them out but I have an idea."

"Make it a good one."

"It is."

"Thanks. Talk to you later."

I roll my window down and let go of the last of the freaking out rage, "MOOOOOOVVVVE. FUCKING MOOOOOVE!"

"HELLO, I'M BAXTER SCHROEDER. I HAD AN APPOINTMENT two hours ago."

I put my hands in my pockets and roam around while a woman in a window disappears. I have my bag full of documents and my confidence is waning.

BAX: I love you so much. I love you so fucking much. I love you more than Costas' baklava. I love you more every moment we exist. More every second of our lives, every leaf, every root, breath and adventure we take. Thank you for so much for choosing me.

TABI: Where the fuck are you?

All my stress breaks as I let out a large laugh. My wife doing the exact thing I should have anticipated her doing.

BAX: I'm just picking up a couple of things, then I'm racing back to you.

TABI: Stop being romantic and get here. I need you.

BAX: I know. But remember, as of tonight, there are things that will need us more.

TABI: I'll always need you the most. Even if this kid turns out to be super needy. I'll be the neediest. I love you. Now, please stop being fucking vague and get your sexy ass here.

BAX: On my way.

"Mr. Schroeder." I turn and two women and a man come into view. I recognize one of the women as the case worker we've worked with before. Becca Gelbert is here. I don't know when she did this and how she knew this was so important to me. I've been freaking out that there might be a hitch when I get here but she knew how important it was. I hug her and she actually hugs me back.

"Who's with Tabi?"

"I got Poppy deputized so she can officially hand over the baby if we don't get there in the next forty minutes. But I wanted to make sure there were no problems here. This matters, Bax. You all matter." A rare moment of sentiment from our resident skeptic. I hug her again and she lets me.

"Fuck." I run my hands through my hair. I look up and all three of them are staring at me. I realize I just swore. "Shit, I'm sorry. Fuck." I put my hands out in front of me. "I promise I'm going to be a better father than my language."

Our case worker smiles and says, "They've been through hell and back, I'm not sure saying the f-word could possibly make you a bad father in their eyes."

She rushes to me, and I extend my hand.

"Nope. Not for this." She hugs me. "You know I think these kids are special, but I can't think of a better Christmas than this. For all of us."

I hand her the folder of all the documents. She smiles. "Just sign all of these, I'll be in touch for a home visit and Becca will get your court date set."

"That's it?"

"That's it."

I'm awash in emotions and a little unstable. I wish Tabi

were here, that we could be in both places at once. "Do they know I'm here?"

Becca grins. "We thought you might want to tell them." She puts out her hand and I take it. I'm glad she's the unemotional one. If anyone else were here I'd be more of a puddle. The tears in my eyes are just sitting there poised to fall. I blink them back and we enter a little room. The boys light up and start screaming. They run to me, I open my arms and am almost knocked over. I pull them to me together. And then one by one.

Jay is crying. Just full-on crying and Joaquin is trying to be brave. He's toughing it out, so I let go. I let the tears flow and by doing so I give him permission to be a sap too.

"No one should be alone on Christmas. Unless you guys want to stay here in this dumpy little room?" They laugh. "I'm so happy to see you two. We've missed you so much." Jay won't let go of me and I keep my arm tight around him.

Joaquin steps back and crosses his arms. "What now, Baxter?"

They don't know that we're not here to foster them.

"First we work on getting your math grade up or your mother will kill you."

Jay says, "She doesn't want us."

I ruffle his hair. "Not that one. The other one. The one who wants you just as much as I do and can't imagine another day without the two of you in our lives. What do you say? Will you have us? Wanna hang around us for like, forever?"

Jay immediately yells, "Yes!"

Joaquin's jaw drops. I open my arms. "Come here, son." And my new brave boy falls to pieces right there on the ground. I rush to him and take him in my arms. Jay joins us in our crying mess.

Joaquin finally calms down, looks at Jay and says, "Best Christmas EVER."

I stand and wipe my eyes. "Well, it's about to get a whole lot crazier if you're up for it."

Jay says, "Is Auntie Elle pregnant again?" Warms my heart he called her Auntie Elle. That they feel connected to our world.

I laugh. "She is, but this is about us. And, get this, Auntie Ingrid has a boyfriend."

"No way. She's back from France?"

"Yes, but more importantly, how do you feel about a baby brother?"

Joaquin raises his eyebrows. "Holy shit. Tabi's pregnant?"

I smile to cover up how much I wish that were true. I don't want them to think we don't want them just as much as a baby we're unable to have. "No. But there's a kid in Oakland who needs you guys and us. He needs a family. And I kind of volunteered you."

Jay says, "Wait. Like this isn't a foster thing?"

Joaquin looks at his brother. "No. I think they're adopting us." He looks at me, and I smile.

Jay says, "That fucking rocks."

"Watch your language. And I'm going to watch mine. I make no promises for your mother. Now, we have to try to get to Oakland in like twenty minutes."

"Wait, we're getting the baby today?"

"Yup."

Jay says, "Then let's go."

Joaquin flings open the door and looks in the hallway. Then gestures. "Let's go, Auntie Becca, we have another brother to pick up." Then he takes her hand, and they walk down the hall. Becca smiles warmly at him. That kid is fucking magic.

We're walking to the car, and I know Tabi's arriving at the

hospital right now. We're not going to make it even remotely. Glancing at my phone I see there's an accident so we have to go around the long way through Richmond, then back through Napa and over to home.

"Tabi doesn't know anything about you guys. You're a surprise."

"Good, cuz I didn't get her nothing for Christmas."

"I didn't get her anything," I correct Jay.

He repeats it back to me. Joaquin says, "Do we still call you Bax?"

"You can call me anything you want."

"Dickhead?"

We all laugh at Jay.

"Funny, but not appropriate."

"Dad," Joaquin says. "That sounds weird."

I say, "To me too. But know that we adore you both and we'll just settle into it." He nods. "I have to call your mother, so you bananas be quiet."

Jay zips his lips and I grin at him in the rearview mirror.

"Hey."

Her voice is panicked and adorable. "Hi. Are you here? Poppy just went to get the kid. I signed our life away. You have to sign stuff too by next week. And Becca's not here. And I don't know what I'm doing. They just handed me some spit cloths and bottles. And formula. Apparently, I'm going to feed the kid." She says all of that in one breath. The boys stifle giggles in the back.

It's killing me. "Mama, you'll be fine. I love you. Take videos, so many videos. Can you kiss the kid for me? I'm not going to be there right now, but for the rest of his days, I will be. So, meet me at home. Hurry home to me. I have something for you that will complete your life."

"A working bathroom and a floor for our bedroom?"

"Better. I'm going to go unless you want me to stay on the line. I'm in traffic south of the city but headed east to get around it. But you should head home."

"Why are you South of San Francisco?"

"Very long story. But it has a happily ever after."

"Then it can be our kid's first bedtime story. You go. I have to focus on fucking transforming into a mother. I love you."

"Love you."

The boys giggle. "She's going to fucking die when she sees us."

I let it go. It's true.

TABI

A nurse has a camera pointed at me and I'm holding all the assorted things when Poppy comes into the room. I drop them. I'm sitting with a nurse and a case worker, and I can't stop my leg from bouncing. I breathe in and touch my tummy. At least I'm not totally alone. She's holding a tiny thing in a white blanket with a blue and pink stripe. He doesn't look like much. His eyes are closed and he's super squishy. And he has a really stupid hat that doesn't fit him right on his head. Why do that to a kid? Start him out in life wearing a beanie.

The nurse nudges me, and I realize I'm supposed to hold him. I've forgotten everything. I hold up my finger and lean over to a tiny garbage can and vomit. I wipe my mouth and outstretch my hands. The nurse rushes to me and cleans them, then pats me on the back. I glance at Poppy and her eyes are wide as she approaches. Her eyes are always wide but there's more wonder in them.

I reach out and she gives me the baby, then I look at her and nod. She starts sobbing and places her hand on my stomach and although it's not 'Gouda' making me sick, somehow, she knows. I nod to her, and she gasps. You better fucking gasp, I mean, this shit is insane.

I look down and pull him close to me and say, "What's up? I'm your mom. Oh my God. I'm your mom. I'm somebody's mom. Don't leave, ok? I'm going to get better at this."

The nurse puts her arm around me. "You're already better at this."

Poppy holds her hands over her heart. "Better than you know."

I look down and it's more than I can bear. Like I want to wrestle the world for him. Make sure no one fucks with him, and he gets everything. The pieces of my own childhood lock into place and I understand everything about Costas and Goldie that I never did before. All of their bullshit was just to protect me.

THE KID IS FED AND CHANGED. HE EVEN OPENED HIS DARK eyes. They're like mine. His hair is dark and sparse like my dad's, and his wide nose is the cutest thing I've ever seen. They tell me his pigmentation will darken over the next month or so. We don't know how dark his skin will get and it really doesn't matter. But there is a little thrill that goes through me again that he's a boy. We settle the nameless kid into his seat and jump in the car.

Traffic is horrific. I take about one thousand pictures, but I don't want to text anyone until he's met his father. I'm holding onto the video so I can be there when he sees him for the first time. I don't even want Bax to see him in a picture before he meets him. He's so fucking cute. I love him so much. My nameless kid. I've been at the hospital for a couple of hours and now it's close to six p.m. I'm never getting home because of traffic. It's too much.

We're about an hour and only two miles into our journey when Poppy sits up a little straighter. The car begins to power down and she eases out of traffic to the sidelines.

"What?" No. This can't be happening. Thank God the kid is sleeping. I'm in the back with him holding his foot. It's my favorite part of him, so far.

"Calm."

"No." I lean forward.

"Calm down, Tabi."

"What is it?" I say with all the calm I can muster and that's not much today.

"Um. You know how, um, sometimes, I forget things."

"Like what?!"

"Like gas."

"Oh shit." I look out the window at the highway and its solid traffic in both directions. There's no way anyone could get to us. Fuck. We're close to an exit, but I can't leave the kid. "My new car is out of gas."

Poppy turns around sheepishly. "I'm so sorry. I'm a mess. I'm a mess about it. I'll make it up to you. I'll walk and get gas."

I can't make her do that. Shit. "Can we call an UBER?" I look at my phone and the closest car is an hour and half away. I have to get back to Sonoma. Bax needs to meet his kid. It's fucking Christmas Eve.

"No car. Um. Think."

"Poppy. Help me get the kid out of the thing."

"Car seat?"

"Yes. That thing."

"What are you doing?"

"I'm going to haul him in this bucket thing, we're going to walk to that exit, find a restaurant, probably puke on the way, and figure this shit out."

"But all the exhaust fumes will hurt him."

"We live in California, in a tinderbox of a wildfire area. His lungs never had a chance."

"I'll carry everything else." She puts up her hood, and I nestle the kid down with the extra blankets. And who knew the hat would come in handy?

She slings the diaper bag over her shoulder and our bags. I start hauling the kid. I take a quick picture of our insane journey to... I look up and the closest exit is Jingletown. Of course, it is. Ho muthafucking ho.

❧ 19 ❧

BAX

"Cover your ears, gentlemen." They do as they're told. "FUCKKKKK. FUCK ME! FUCKING FUCK." I can't even get home. I just shoved some McDonald's down their throats. Some fucking father I'm turning out to be. What a delightful Christmas Eve dinner. I'm not there to meet my one son and these two have zero nutrition—although I did make them eat the apple slices—and have nowhere to sleep or a mother right now.

My phone rings. I glance at the boys and nod. They uncover their ears.

Jay says, "You know that didn't work. We heard you. You're swearing like Tabi now."

"Watch your mouth."

We all laugh. I answer.

"BAX. It's Elle."

"What's up? Do I have a bed yet?"

"By the way, everyone knows, except Tabi. Your dad and

Sam are lousy secret keepers. Your sisters are madly baking cookies for them. Hi Jay! Joaquin! Merry Christmas!"

They yell their response, "Merry Christmas, Auntie Elle!"

She squeals, "Are you close?"

"No. And is Tabi there?" I pull into a different lane with the goal of taking winding surface streets instead of the I-80 nightmare.

"Not yet. Did you talk to her?"

"No and I'm going out of my skin. She hasn't answered me in an hour. I don't even know if she has our son."

"She does, but I heard that from Poppy. But no worries, she forbids Poppy from sending or taking any pictures." I smile and my heart fills. She wants me to see him live. Or to be the first or whatever. "Just hurry. And meet Josh at Pro/Ho real quick when you get in town."

"We're still open?"

"Yes, but he's confused on the new inventory system, and we'll never have a decent Christmas if he's thinking he messed something up. Ok. Hurry. There's a whole army of people who can't wait to see you, J&J!"

Joaquin says, "Tell the aunts that Jay's allergic to peanut butter."

"Noted. And they've altered all recipes to include cashew butter. We got you."

Jay yells, "BEST CHRISTMAS EVER!"

Elle laughs and hangs up. I turn back to him. "Totally agree, little man." I reach back and they both grab my hand. I don't pull it away and we drive on.

I try again. "Siri, call Bee."

"Why do you call her Bee?"

"Because when we were younger than both of you, I made a joke of her name. And called her Tabeeeetha, then shortened it to Bee."

"Is that why she has a bee tattoo on her wrist?"

I put both hands on the wheel and pull up my left sleeve and hold my matching one up for them to see. The result of a double dog dare from my wife a year ago.

Joaquin says, "Can we get one too?"

"I'm going to go with a no. No tattoos for Christmas. Or for your entire childhood."

"Really, man?"

I laugh, "Yes, really. Hard no."

"But..."

"Nope. But how about we put bees on the Prohibition property, and you can learn how to harvest honey?"

Jay says, "That does not seem fun."

Joaquin says, "I don't know. Maybe."

I'll take that. I turn on the radio and they groan as Barry Manilow's Christmas album gives me life.

20

TABI

J ingletown is a magical place with a bright-ass Army/Navy
store and a beautiful winter village gas station on every
corner. No. But it does appear to be an arts district and
it's decked out in a million white lights.

I slog up the exit and my phone tumbles down the on-ramp
and into traffic. Fucking magical. I was going to call Bax and
let him know what's happened. Shit. Shit. Shit. Thank God for
the photo cloud.

Ok, I need to get my kid to some shelter. I need to actually
provide a life for him the way the parents thought I could. I'm
in a mess and have no way to fix it. Think, Tab. We crest the
exit and cross the street. We walk a couple of blocks in silence.
I have no idea where I'm wandering to, just keep moving. The
houses are dotted with inflatable snowmen and rigid plastic
reindeer. It's kitschy but not tacky. There's something so
earnest in their endeavor to spread cheer.

I angle the bucket so he can see the decorations. One

house is blaring "Hark the Herald Angels Sing" from it, and Poppy and I join in. Neither of us are good but it lifts us up for a moment. The kid's eyes are bright and he's just squirming a little. I'd like to think he's dancing.

I look towards the buildings clustered ahead, and it is actually magical. There's art everywhere. The tiniest tiny boy is waking up for real and we find a bench. He's screeching. It's cute. If this is baby crying, I can manage this no problem. I find his little pacifier, stick my finger in it and put it back in his mouth. He sucks on my finger through the plastic.

"Dude. We have to get home."

Poppy flops onto the bench. "This is awful but at least it's a pretty place."

"Ok, what do we do now?" I ask.

"We could look at the murals." Poppy says brightly as if that's fucking helping.

I roll my eyes. "We have to get home. I dropped my phone and it skidded onto the 880. I know you're savvier than this. Figure this out. I'm too busy mothering. You're the deputy, fucking do something."

"Don't yell at me." Her phone springs to life.

"Sorry."

"Hi." I hear a deep man's voice. "How did you know? Never mind. I don't want to know how many trackers are on me." Her voice has a lilt to it. I ignore it. I unstrap my kid and hold him to me. I smell him. Damn, that's a good smell. I kiss his teeny, little forehead that's peeking out. I also smell his butt and make sure he's good in that department. Then I tighten the burrito wrapper around him and put him back in the bucket.

"Ok. Me too."

"You know it's ok, I know you're together." I sling my arm around Poppy.

She grins. "No, it's not. Follow me." She jumps up and I follow. Suddenly she's got it all figured out but isn't sharing the journey.

I'm not sure what else can go wrong today on a day that everything was supposed to go right. Shit. I'm nauseous again. I pass the bucket to Poppy and bolt over to a garbage can. I puke and dry heave. A hand rubs my back, and I let her. I don't think about it, but it's nice. Then I glance to the side and Poppy's staring at me with her face in a frozen expression of concern. I look behind me and stiffen up. I turn and a homeless Santa in a bedraggled suit is rubbing my back.

"Oh, man, that's so sweet of you. But I'm good."

He says with his four teeth, "Mighty fine babe you got there all wrapped up in them swaddling clothes."

"Thanks." I move between Poppy and Street Santa. "We're going to keep him." Poppy steps back. I smile at him. "Can I get you something, Santa?"

"No. I just heard the baby noises and wanted to see and maybe sing a bit about him. Mighty fine babe. Mighty fine."

"Ok, cool. Merry Christmas, Santa?" I don't know what he wants to be called. "I've always loved 'Silent Night.' How about you sing that?" I back away from him, confused what this is about.

"Sounds perfect. But do you know where you're going?"

"Yup, we're all set."

Poppy says, "Actually if you could tell us how to get to Peterson and East 7th?" I whip my head around to her. She shrugs.

Street Santa pulls up his mottled crimson britches and scratches under the tatters of his hat.

"Now I don't know nothing about slouching towards Bethlehem, but if you folks wander on over towards that purple building, the one with the star on the side, and take a left that will put you on Peterson."

Poppy grins. "Which direction?"

He points. "East."

I nod and he starts singing "Star of Wonder." Fuck, I wish I had my phone.

"Poppy. Can you take a picture of us?" This guy is a little off kilter, but he won't hurt us. And this is the kid's first adventure. I grab the bucket and take my child's first picture with Santa. And he didn't even cry.

⚜

POPPY (TABI): IT'S ME. THE CAR RAN OUT OF GAS ON THE fucking 880. And my phone now lives there. It was smashed by a piece-of-shit Kia minivan.

BAX: Holy shit! Are you ok? Where have you been?

POPPY (TABI): Me? I just told you where I've been. What fucking city business puts you in traffic south of SF? What the hell is going on?

BAX: I love you. Is he ok?

POPPY (TABI): Stop distracting me with romance. He's perfect. He met Santa.

BAX: I'm home. I'm home now. Get to me. Get to me fast.

POPPY (TABI): Working on it. Apparently, there's some plan in place. And I think I know who is moving the pieces. I'm grateful for his shady resources and my excitable redhead prophet.

BAX: We're all waiting on you.

We walk another six blocks, and the buildings and murals fascinate both of us and my worry slips a little. Until we're standing in an industrial, but slowly gentrifying, part of the neighborhood as it starts to get dark. Yes, there are Christmas lights but I'm not so sure we should be out on the streets of an Oakland neighborhood in an unpopulated area with a five-day-old baby as our only defense. What are we going to do, yell "Look how cute he is, please don't take our wallets?"

"Pop. What the hell are we doing?"

She doesn't even hesitate. She's a straight arrow that one. Give her a direction and she takes it to the letter.

"Why are we in front of a warehouse?"

"Come with me." She moves to the doorway and pushes a black button. Then a small green light comes on and she lines up her eyes.

"What the hell?"

"Don't ask questions I can't answer." She smiles as the door swings open and skips inside. "Come on."

Inside is a large, empty warehouse with one light on. And thankfully it's a bathroom.

I take the bucket with me and Poppy twirls around the space like we're in some fucking fairy land.

My kid is five days old in a dusty old warehouse, never met his father and our only company is Mary Fucking Poppins.

"I swear you hear a way different drummer than the rest of us."

She dusts off a chair and sits, crossing her legs at the ankles. "Takes one to know one."

I nod. "I'm going to change the kid and pee."

"Hurry. Our ride will be here in..." She looks at her phone. "Seven minutes."

I take the changing pad out and place it on a strange metal drawer thing in the bathroom. Then pull out the kid. We stare at each other a little too long. It's my first solo flight with his ass and I think we're both unprepared for it.

I manage to get the diaper off and, much to my surprise, it doesn't quite stink. But it is kind of all over his tiny butt.

I yell, "Poppy, google black, green tar coming out of a baby's ass."

"I'm not prepared for you to be a mother," she yells back.

"Me neither, but here we are." I look down at the kid and wipe him clean. Then I kiss his little belly and he pees on my face. Kind of gross but a good note for the future. I'll have to tell Bax not to do this. Or maybe I'll forget and wait for it to happen to him.

"Also, he just pissed on my face."

"Black, green goop totally normal. And wash your face." I move to the sink, then retreat back to him. Fuck. I can't just leave him on a thing. That's new. I try and think of others first, especially Bax, but this is other level.

I get a diaper on him, and it looks nothing like it should, but I use some extra tabs off another diaper to make sure it's all stuck together. I manage to wash my face and neck while still keeping a grip on the kid. He makes a sweet noise, and my heart opens wider than I thought possible.

"Hi. I'm sorry about this day. But I'm pretty glad you won't remember it. I'm going to fuck up a lot, but never doubt that I love you already." I kiss his little feet. They're seriously the best.

A very loud noise is happening all around us. "TAB! We have to go." It's an intense whirring sound like a hundred industrial fans just came to life.

I reswaddle the child and put him in his bucket thing. I collect all the stuff, except the diaper, then there's a big chuchunk noise as something lands on the roof.

I raise my eyebrows to Poppy who's descending a staircase with headphones in her hand.

She hands one to me with a microphone attached, and a small pair of what appears to be a noise-cancelling device and places it on my son. My son. That's the first time I thought that. I like it.

We climb the stairs and standing in front of a helicopter with his arms crossed in front of his massive body, is a six-foot-five, dark haired Italian man with questionable morals and connections. I grin at our electric sleigh. He gestures to the two of us.

I speak Italian to him, "Non puoi fare a meno di essere l'eroe, vero fratello?"

"Your Italian's rusty, but I think you called me a hero and your brother. Now get your ass in the fucking chopper. This is costing me more than your fucking car."

"The car you forgot to fill with gas?"

Someone lifts Poppy into the copter, then she leans down to get the bucket. I hoist myself in, followed by the man who takes up all the space in almost any room he enters. Even if he wasn't a mafia don, that power would still radiate from him. He gestures to the pilot and another man.

"This is Frank and Murray."

"Does that make you gold?"

"Nah, that one's fucking gold." He gestures to the baby. "I'm just a wise guy with some money who's taking you back to the fucking manger."

We all strap in, and the bucket wobbles a bit. Sal takes the baby out and gestures to me, and I smile and nod to him. He cuddles him close in his Buick-bumper-sized biceps. He has lots of nieces and nephews, but I had a suspicion he'd be a natural. I settle back in my seat as the three wise guys return me to Bax.

Sal says, "We need to get you home, my sorellina." He calls me his little sister. I glare at him, and he laughs.

"Home. That's funny." I have no home. Sal winks and Poppy

giggles, then curls into his side. She glances up at me and I grin at her. She shrugs and kisses Sal in front of me for the first time. It's amazing. Everything is amazing. Except my lost phone, lost mind and lost husband. I start to panic and then the baby yawns. Like the tiniest, little mouth opens and does something completely human and adult. I won't fall apart because he needs me, but if he sneezes, I'm going to lose it. I reach over and touch his tiny cheek. Sal makes to transfer him back to me, but I shake my head no.

"He's completely comfortable right where he is, let's not fuck with it."

Sal's lip curls up and he says, "Mouth of an Angel."

"I'm trying." I shrug.

Poppy reaches over and squeezes my forearm. "You're succeeding." Her voice is reedy and positive through my headphones.

I sit back and let all of this wash over me. I look out the window and hope to God wherever the hell we land, Bax is there. Poppy lifts her phone to show me.

POPPY: We're on our way.

BAX: We're here and ready.

POPPY: Like fifteen minutes. {PICTURE OF TABI KISSING THE BABY ON THE HEAD.}

BAX: Thank you. I'll never be able to thank you both enough. Bring me my wife and baby safely, please.

POPPY (TABI): I love you and this baby who has no name. I didn't pick one. I'm not even thinking of one. I couldn't. Because I'm waiting. Will you wait for me to do it?

BAX: Always.

I've never been in a helicopter. It's loud and I'm grateful for his tiny headphones that somehow Sal found. He's sleeping fine. Good to know in case Bax and I are ever rested enough to have loud dirty sex again. I'm going to hold onto the headphones and if the baby can't sleep, we'll just put him in a helicopter.

I can't take my eyes off him. He's doing nothing, but I need to make sure he keeps breathing. Sal's just staring at him as well. Then we start to descend, and Poppy begins clapping as she looks out the window. I think there's going to be a helipad, but I look down and our regulation basketball court at Prohibition is bright as anything with a giant red and white circle of Christmas lights.

They made a helipad. The barn at Pro/Ho, our offices et cetera, are a beacon in the dark. My head whips between the three of them and they start laughing. The barn is draped in Christmas lights. I mean covered. They even decorated our condemned collapsed house.

I'm going home. They created a home at my home. As we land, I see every tree is lit up and my eyes scan for the one thing I need to see to feel centered, grounded and ready to be a fucking mother. I scan the crowd—it's all of them. It's everyone in my life. It's the 5 Families all holding those orange cone things and waving. My mom is being held back by Will Whittier, Josh's dad. And Elle waves and points to something over to the side.

We land and Sal hands me my son and slides the door open. There's music. There's Christmas carols playing by a band headed by Sam. There are people everywhere. There's love and joy, and I can't even focus and breathe until he's in my face kissing me quickly, then pulling the baby to his chest. Someone helps me out and then I'm in his arms, the baby between us. He kisses me again, and I push the tears away. There's yelling and screaming but all of it fades as he pulls the little blanket back, and two deep brown eyes blink up at us.

"Hi, Nick. I'm your dad."

My eyes meet his. "Nick? Like Yia Yia's Nick?" He nods. I

can't believe he remembered my grandfather, who he never met. But we're Greek, it was a pretty safe bet that I'd be related to a Nick.

"Or St. Nick, whichever you prefer."

I grin. "Nicholas Harris," I say.

Bax kisses me quickly when I tell him our baby's middle name is his mother's maiden name. As much as I'd love to saddle him with the name Bellamy, I figure this is enough tribute to the woman we'll always wish he could have met.

I look up and Goldie is yelling. "That's my baby. That is one of my babies. My life is so full tonight. You darling brave girl. I could bust open a pineapple with my teeth I'm so happy." My mother is babbling. I turn and Costas is a blubbering mess.

"Pops, you gotta pull it together."

I take the baby from Bax and place him in my father's arms. And he sobs even harder.

"Ok. Let's all calm the hell down. It's just a baby."

My father says, "No. It's a family for a girl who tried hardest to have one. And now you do." The word washes over me, and I feel like laser beams are shooting out of me. Costas turns and holds Nick up like he's in the fucking *Lion King*. And all my extended family cheer.

Bax pulls me to the side and holds me. Then he turns me back toward the crazy lit-up barn. He says in my ear, "Elle outfitted the barn with a living room, bedrooms, and there's even a new fridge just for us. We can live there until we figure it out. There's space for all of us."

I pull his arms around me tighter. "So, we're living in a manger?"

"Yup. But there's one more thing I need to tell you."

"Is it how you fucked up today and weren't with me? And

my phone got run over by traffic and we don't have our new pretty car, and it's all your fault?"

"Yes. Exactly that."

He turns me towards the corner of the crowd and my eyes drift over to David and Natalie. She leans down and my jaw goes slack. This is a mirage. Natalie nudges two of the most amazing things I'll ever see, and they all-out sprint towards us.

Bax kisses my cheek and says, "Merry Christmas. Am I forgiven?"

"MOM!! MOM!!"

I look to Becca, and she has her hands over her heart. She squeezes my shoulder and says, "These are yours again. For keeps. No take backs."

I'm frozen in time and space as Joaquin and Jay swallow me whole in a flurry of hugs and joyous yells. Jay is crying.

"I missed you fuckers."

Joaquin looks at Bax. "I told you, Dad. She's never going to keep her mouth under control." Then he pauses. "Is it ok that I call you Dad?"

I answer, "Did you just call me Mom?"

Jay says, "That's what you are. You're not sending us back, ever. That's what Bax, I mean, Dad said. We get to stay. And that you love us and we love you. Or I do. I don't know about Joaquin."

Baxter steps to us. I look up at everyone all around us and that's when I remember I have a secret too.

"Did you idiots meet your brother?"

BAX

I'm not sure what I expected—that she'd magically become someone else. But no, she's exactly as I would expect and want. We'll just have to teach our children not to use the language their mother does. Goldie runs back toward us, away from the crowd. I haven't moved from the spot where we became a family.

"Mister Baxter, the big poppa. Here is your little dreamy one. I'll try not to hold him too much. Adrian, look at our grandbaby." My father nods to Goldie and kisses the top of his dear friend's head.

I kiss my mother-in-law on the cheek and reach for Nick. There's a hand on my shoulder, firm and always at my back. My father takes the baby from Goldie. He's a patient man, steady and true. I've always tried to emulate him at least in spirit. He looks at the baby and I see Tabi running around with the other boys.

"Dad."

He nods at me and says, "Dad."

I grin. "Meet Nicholas"

"I heard. Nick. I like it."

"Nicholas Harris Schroeder." My father looks up from Nick's little sleeping face.

"Well, son, that's a good name. She'd like that." My father misses my mom every day. Someday I hope he'll date again, but for now I have a hunch he'll be busy with Nick as often as possible. My sisters and their significant others crowd around my dad and more pictures are taken. I kiss my new son's head and wave to everyone and go to find the rest of my family. That is still knocking the wind out of me when I say or think it.

I see David, Josh and Sam huddled in the corner of our new quasi residence. I walk over and they stare at me with their eyes wide.

Josh says, "Dude. That's a lot."

Sam chimes in, "Says the man with a fourth child on the way."

David sips and says ribbing Josh about the unexpected twins he already has, "You hope it's just a fourth."

We all laugh, and David throws his arms around me. "I'm so fucking happy for you, man." Then Sam and Josh take their turns.

Sam says, "I can't believe I kept all the secrets. Kind of. I kept them from Tabi."

"They're all out now. Thanks, man, for holding it together."

Sam says, "Seriously, I was ok keeping the foster kid thing, but fucking Tabi, man. It's why I didn't speak to you today."

"What are you talking about?" I ask, worried now something's wrong.

David and Josh reach over to tackle Sam to the ground, and I block them.

"Tell me now." I look around and Tabi's missing.

"About the baby."

"I know about the baby."

Sam, oblivious to David and Josh struggling to stop him from talking, says, "No, the other one." Fuck. My breath is gone, and Josh puts his hands on my shoulders before I kill Sam for being an idiot.

I spin around quickly to find her face. She's standing with a Santa suit clad Will Whittier who's dancing with his oldest granddaughter. I catch her attention, my eyes wide, and my body is humming with, well, to be honest, panic. How the fuck do we do this? This can't be true. David slams into Sam, and he realizes what he did. How does everyone know but me?

Tabi stomps over. She yells, "Fuckface asshole!" She stabs Sam in the chest.

He shakes her off. "Such fucking drama. Whatever. Stop telling me shit." David puts his hand on his arm, and he shakes him off. "Fuck off. Merry Christmas. I'm out." He stomps off, and I could care less.

I grab the woman of all my dreams and pull her to me. "Is this true?"

She grins and places her hand on her stomach. I kiss the hell out of her. We're never going to have time together after today.

She says into my ear, "Healthy. Four months along. The doctor called today after they checked me out last night. But I went for an ultrasound."

"You know I missed all of that. I don't want to miss a moment of anything."

"We have three kids and a fourth on the way, we're going to miss shit. But I'll try and remember you want to be around. Merry Christmas."

"Hell of a present."

She looks over my shoulder and my sister, Ingrid, and her boyfriend, Ian, are running around with her new nephews.

Tabi says, "They certainly are." Then she looks around. "Where the hell is the baby?"

"Someone in our family has him. He's fine."

"I need your phone?" She reaches in my pants pocket. I'm confused, everyone we know is here and there's plenty of people taking pictures. Then it dawns on me.

"You put those airport people in my phone, didn't you?"

"Yeah. I did."

"Fine, but we have things to do. We have a lot of presents to wrap for them and eventually, we're going to need to lay that babe in swaddling clothes down in his makeshift manger." She kisses me, then we both look as we hear Goldie screaming and running.

"I got the baby bottom duty. I do it. Boys, fall in line with Yia Yia Goldie. We'll work as a team to get the baby bottom clean as the whistles. Come. Come. Eláte agapitoí mou." She has the baby in one arm and grabs Jay's hand with Joaquin following close behind.

Joaquin asks, "Goldie Yeah Yeah?"

"Yia Yia." She looks back at the boys.

"We don't know what you said."

"You will. Greek lessons start back up next week. What a wonderful present for you two. But I said, come my dear ones." Jay hugs her and Joaquin rolls his eyes. That's the one that will take after Tabi.

She looks back to me and says, "Do you think we'll ever see our kids?"

I kiss her. "Let's move somewhere where no one knows us."

She laughs a little too hard. "Then what would we do? I'd have to constantly fly back here to check on Costas and Goldie."

"Yia Yia's got them." She laughs at my joke.

I say, "I'll be back in a second."

"Take your time. I'll be in with our flock of boys if anyone will let me get to them."

She winks at me, and she's just as fucking gorgeous and sexy as she's always been, but now, she is growing our child and running a winery, and she's grown into the most complete and beautiful Tabi. I turn to our makeshift house and David's mom who was supposed to host this party smiles at me. She loves Christmas and I'm positive all this décor is hers. Elle's waddling around holding one of her baby girls and wearing a slim-cut mermaid wedding dress with a giant pouch for her belly.

I walk up and kiss her on the cheek. "You're amazing. Thank you. Thank you so much. You're our Christmas angel."

"What can I say? I like fixing things, throwing events and wearing white dresses. I was born to do this. Oh and I love pulling off miracles when all hope is gone. I'm a multitude of the heavenly host." Her blonde hair swings at her shoulders when she turns from me.

A deep voice comes up behind her, "Is that why you're wearing white?" Josh scoops up the baby girl and now he's holding the twins on his shoulders. He kisses Elle. "Because it ain't cuz you're virginal." She glares at him. "Hellcat, don't give me that look, you know what happens when you give me that look." He puts his hand on her belly and kisses her sweetly.

I say to the two of them, "One day, four kids. We have four kids. We have four kids in less than twenty-four hours."

Tabi says behind me, "And I hope you have a lot of money saved up for us because we have lots of mouths to feed, and I don't need you wrapping yourself up in stress."

"Your chaos is the only thing I ever want to be wrapped up in. Merry Christmas."

22

TABI

"**M**erry Christmas to you, my sneaky bastard husband. I might need a word with the Senator in a little bit." I purse my lips and look at my gorgeous husband. "Or maybe I'll just dream of him for months, because I'm pretty sure that's how long I'm going to sleep."

"Anything you say, Bee." He kisses me and it's more suggestive than I have bandwidth for but it's nice. Flirting I can manage, sex, maybe in like three years.

"Anything?" I raise an eyebrow.

"Within reason, we *are* parents now, tying you up might bring on a couple of questions."

"Bring them on!" Or maybe the challenge of trying to have it all will be my next great adventure. Perhaps a parental Fuckit list is in order? I can fill it with things we can do to each other when children go to bed. Noise cancelling headphones for the lot of them!

Bax dips his head to mine and attacks my lips. This kiss is heated and driving. It's also soulful and uniting. His tongue brushes against mine and I lick back into his mouth. He crushes me closer, and I hear a cry. My body instantly lets the desire for him ebb away. I turn and my mom hands me my new son.

"His bottom clean, his belly full, but yet he cries. So now it's time for a mama's love to make him stop." Goldie turns away from me and begins to walk away from a crying baby.

"You're just leaving me with him."

My mom turns back and kisses me on the cheek. "You will be terrible at this, and then, like everything else in your Tabitha life, you will soar like the eagles on the wind."

She pinches my cheek, and I start bouncing with the baby the way I've seen Josh or David calm their kids. I walk away and start making those shushing sounds. He stops. I made him stop. I'm a fucking genius at this. Then he starts again. I bounce and he stops. Shit. Does that mean I have to keep bouncing until my calves burn? He's snuggled into one arm. I experiment with left-handed, one-armed texting.

BAX (TABI): Here's something.

TRISTAN: Please identify yourself, this is a foreign number.

BAX (TABI): It's me, assholes. My phone's roadkill. I just wanted to send you all a quick Schroeder/Aganos Christmas card of the fam. {Picture of baby, Bax and the boys.}

SABRINA: Are those THE boys?

RORY: That's a right good Xmas if I ever saw one.

BAX (TABI): Yes. They're ours again, permanently.

JONATHAN: That's just about the greatest freaking thing I've ever seen. You're a mama of three now? And yesterday you were just someone who wrecked their house with sex?

BEN: Well, done. Top drawer for all of you. Smashing. Seriously well done the lot of you. Happy Christmas and good tidings for all.

SABRINA: *Bax is really hot. I mean like otherworldly hot.*

BAX (TABI): *I know.*

JONATHAN: *Had no idea he was blond or that I was your type.*

TABI: *Hmm. He's a blond who essentially grew up on a farm. It's a shame he's my soul mate and I met him when we were five years old. You could have had a shot at all this, farm boy.*

TRISTAN: *Sherilynn is sobbing. She's thrilled for you and the bizarre birth of baby Shona. Love and kindness to all. Tabi what's his name.*

TABI: *Nick. After my grandfather. And Jay and Joaquin. I think Joaquin should take my last name. I think Schroder is too much. Aganos sounds better. Nick can take his last name.*

RORY: *Please stop talking to us and be with your family.*

TABI: *Look who's talking.*

RORY: *It's the middle of the night here. Zoe and family are asleep. Well, all but one. {Picture of tiny redhead girl wide awake in a giant bicep.}*

TABI: *Your arms are truly scary. Are we sure that kid's not terrified of those tree trunks?*

SABRINA: *They are large. Rory, admit it. The baby looks like it's the size of a thimble. You're not to scale.*

RORY: *Goodnight, all.*

TRISTAN: *That's it. No quip or dig at Tabi. No grumpy sign off?*

RORY: *What's there to be grumpy about?*

JONATHAN: *Merry Christmas, everyone.*

BEN: *I was just thinking, Tabi's gone and gotten herself a boy and Rory a girl, perhaps in twenty years or so...*

BAX (TABI): *NO*

RORY: *Absolutely, no.*

SABRINA: *You had to go and rile them up.*

BEN: *Apologies. Carry on, everyone. But will you all be attending the wedding?*

TRISTAN: *I'm going to need an arsenal of nannies I suppose?*

TABI: *The whole Aganos/Schroeder tribe will be there.*

RORY: *We'll be there, but that's too many bloody people from California.*

TABI: *Fuck off Nessie and Happy Christmas.*

SABRINA: *Happy Christmas indeed.*

RORY: *{Picture of Brad's Santa hat on Rory's head and the baby snuggled on his bicep.}*

BEFORE I RETURN TO MY FAMILY AND THE INSANITY OF MY extended family—who are now all dancing around the makeshift helipad, even David's asshole of a father is dancing and singing with his granddaughter—there's one more thing I have to do.

BAX (TABI:) *I'm four months and it's healthy.*

RORY: *I thought it was a bit too easy to get off the line with you.*

BAX (TABI): *Seems like it's going to stick around. I mean I don't know what the future holds, but I do hope I get to meet this baby.*

RORY: *I'll tell you what the future holds: noise, chaos, and utter pandemonium.*

BAX (TABI): *That's it?*

RORY: *And so much fucking joy. The way I feel about Shona, and now you're about to have all of this four times over, Christ, woman, you must be crawling out of your skin.*

BAX (TABI): *Yup. Joy.*

RORY: *What was it we all toasted to in February? To finding our lids. Being stuck in an airport with the lot of you wasn't the worst fucking thing to ever happen.*

BAX (TABI): *Admit it. I'm your best friend.*

RORY: *Fuck no.*

BAX (TABI): *I am.*

RORY: *No, Charlie is.*

BAX (TABI): *Bullshit.*

RORY: Perhaps. Now bugger the hell off. You've no time to mess about with me when there's a gaggle of children now in your care. Heaven help them.

I look up and hear him. Elle sweeps over. "My turn." I grin and hand her Nick, and she floats off in yet another wedding dress. This one has an awfully long train dragging though the dust and dirt. She may hate being pregnant, but she loves fashion and she's so beautiful. Also, how many fucking wedding dresses did my nutbag friend purchase?

I look at Bax and there's a smile in his eyes. One of satisfied terror. I'm sure I look the same. We have no idea how to do this, where we're going to live or what we're going to do. He snaps a picture of me with his city of Sonoma Mayor phone as I give him the finger.

"Get off the phone, now woman." Bax crooks his finger to me.

BAX (TABI): Gotta go get laid, see ya.

RORY: HA! I will never get used to your mouth.

BAX (TABI): Yeah, you will. Someday it will roll off your enormous, muscled back and right down your kilt.

RORY: GO!

BAX (TABI): Kiss that baby for me.

RORY: Same.

Bax takes me in his arms and kisses me. I can't believe what a difference twenty-four hours can make. But looking in his endless blue eyes, I know that whatever bullshit happens with our new pack of wild beasts, we'll tame them together. He takes my hand and leads me back toward J&J. They look tired, and I guide them to say goodnight. Bax's father asks if he can read *The Night Before Christmas* to his new grandchildren.

"Only if we can listen too, Dad," Bax says.

I get the boys ready and snuggled into their insanely comfortable, brand-new beds, tucked into the room that was going to become Sam and David's gym. It's actually pretty great in here. Elle decorated it with Warriors' posters and cars. It looks like a boy's room, not some makeshift lean-to, which is what I thought I'd be sleeping in this evening.

Bax's father, Adrian, puts a chair between their two beds and opens a book.

Bax whispers to me, "I didn't know he still owned that book. It was mom's." I grin. I'm pretty much going to do that a hell of a lot more. Maybe. But I am grateful, all the cups runneth over.

There are Christmas lights all around us, and Adrian shuts out the side lamp. The room glows with the season. I'll never have another day like this, and I just want to remember every irritating, disastrous, wonderful moment.

Then the room begins to fill. First with Goldie and Costas who move close to Joaquin. Ingrid comes in with baby Nick and sits on the end of Jay's bed near me. Her boyfriend, Ian, takes a space on the wall. Next, Tommi, Bax's other sister and her wife enter with their boy. And take up all the space on Joaquin's bed next to Bax. The others are around the door, but it's just my actual family in this room.

He begins but doesn't need the book. Bax, Tommi and Ingrid mouth along and whisper. This must be their thing. My father reaches down to Joaquin and brushes hair from his forehead, and he smiles at him. Rory was right. I'm crawling out of my skin. It's bursting all around me. I know this shit is going to be hard. I know it's not a fucking fairy tale but right here, right now, I'm not sure there will ever be a more perfect moment with my family than this one. Bax catches my eye, and I grin. He puts a hand over his heart and mouths the words, "I love you, Bee."

I mouth back, "Thank you. For all of this. I love you too."

And then I almost throw up because I'm such an emotional

sap. And I'm pretty freaking glad no one can see me but the people in this room. And they know I'd kill them if they told anyone that tears are streaming down my face. Elle once told me she leaks joy sometimes. I guess I do now too.

Adrian's voice is strong and true, just like his son's. And I hope our sons will find that same confidence and sense of self.

"Now, dash away, dash away, dash away, all."

THE END

EPILOGUE

February 12 (the next year) – Chicago, IL
Girl and The Goat Restaurant
2:35 pm US CST

TABI

The wind is whipping the bitter ass snow outside of this window. It keeps curling up into a wave then dispersing when it smacks into something. This city's weather is no joke, and I don't love it here. But my heart is warm and full this Valentine's Day with all the people who are about to show up.

"Well, Bree was not exaggerating. You are quite the loud woman. And you're huge. Sabrina didn't mention you were pregnant. Please God let you be pregnant and not just enormous."

"How dare you?"

"Please." He purses his lips and sarcasm is dripping off his lips. He's a good call for Sabrina.

"It is indeed a baby. A girl to be exact and I have no fucking clue how to raise a girl. I'm pretty amazing at raising boys so far but a girl, no thanks."

"I think it might do you some good to have a touch more estrogen around you, you seem a bit masculine." He laughs at his own joke, and I don't hate him. Patrick smiles and sips the wine I forced him to order so I could smell it.

"You're funnier than I thought you'd be, and that voice is so much more than she let on. I mean she mentioned it was a panty melter but, Jesus, Patrick that's a smooth, slick timbre you got going there."

He laughs again then gulps a big sip of his wine then offers me a smell. I snort it in like a hit. I really do miss wine. Gouda's growing surprisingly good now and it's my last Pro/Ho sales call until who the hell knows. I've been using them as excuses to leave the noise of the boys and sleep excessively. I secretly think Bax likes it. I'm kind of bitchy lately.

I'm only in town for less than a day and I only have these forty-five minutes and the assholes are late. I've been keeping Gouda under wraps, old habit of being terrified of a miscarriage but we're all healthy. And now I'm just terrified because she's a girl. Maybe I'll get lucky, and she'll be a lesbian. I understand that energy, feminine is a mystery to me.

BEN: Are you going to send pictures? This is so exciting. Wish I was there.

TABI: You want a picture of a harried mom and Patrick the wonder voice because those assholes are late?

TRISTAN: We're just minutes away. Settle your arse down.

SABRINA: Tell Patrick I'm sorry.

TABI: Nope. You do that. I'm going to tell him you ditched him for the Schlong.

BEN: Pronounced Schleen.

RORY: Christ, was that just a year ago?

JONATHAN: I'll be there in fifteen. I know there's a tight time-line, but our train just got in. Juliet's with me and she's huge and hungry. Order a lot of bread. Wait until you see my gorgeous pregnant woman.

RORY: Pregnant you say, loud annoying woman. Is this your big reveal or are you still a bloody chicken?

TRISTAN: Reveal?

BEN: I feel a bit lost.

SABRINA: Aren't you always?

BEN: Good point.

RORY: Come on, Tab, show us a pretty picture of you and Patrick. Right now. Full body picture. I bloody dare you.

TABI: Fuck off, Kilt. {Picture of Patrick pointing at a very pregnant Tabi.}

SABRINA: HOLY SHITBALL YOU HAVE SECRETS! And you told my boyfriend first?

TABI: No, I told the asshole in Scotland first then Patrick.

BEN: Blessings.

TRISTAN: You couldn't wait two minutes?

TABI: Nah. Why do things that are expected? And thanks Ben.

JONATHAN: Tristan, you're going to need more nannies at your wedding in July.

RORY: Signing off, I'm knackered. And my work here is done.

BEN: Same. But Laurie and I are over the moon for you Tabi. And holy shit that means you have four children since I've last spent time with you.

TABI: I don't half ass anything.

RORY: Don't sell yourself short, you're a full ass.

TRISTAN: We're here.

TABI: I'm in the back.

Suddenly I'm attacked from behind and lifted out of my chair by a tall and normally very put together British man and a tiny cheerleader squeezes my middle. I notice a small handcuff tattoo on her wrist. I glance over at Patrick and see it mirrored on his wrist.

"What the fuck?" I say and try to get out of their grip.

Tristan kisses my cheek and says, "I believe that's the first thing you ever said to us a year ago. Happy Anniversary, darling."

Sabrina kisses Patrick then says, "Well then, let's turn this shit into a show." I laugh and squeeze her again. She puts her hand on my belly and I place mine over hers. I'm so incredibly grateful for being stuck in the airport, because you never know when you'll pick up more members of your tribe.

Tristan sits and says, "And you promise you're coming back to Kentucky for our wedding? Newborn in hand?"

I grin as my heart overflows with affection. A side effect of pregnancy and having kids, I feel way too fucking much. "Even a disaster couldn't keep me away."

Sabrina pipes up, "Well, I think we've all had enough disasters for the year. I think your wedding will go off without a hitch." She nods her head resolutely as if she's surer of herself in life now.

Tristan raises his glass, and we all follow suit, "Cheers to that and cheers to a year without disasters."

"Amen." I echo his sentiment, but they weren't all disasters. It might just have been our paths leading us to our happily ever afters.

The end...

Thanks so much for being a part of our year of Holiday Disasters.

Evie and I cherish every review and reader that came along this insane journey of ours. We hope we made you smile and laugh and lightened your load just a touch. You've all certainly done that for us. As this project comes to an end, for now, we have one last gift to the Holiday Disasters Volume One – There's an ultimate epilogue in the form of a novelette that will be part of the Volume One Box set releasing in 2023. We couldn't resist one more holiday, Tristan and Sherilyn's wedding.

Consider this your save the date and watch out for your invitation to the wedding that should be a complete disaster.

But in the meantime...

More Rory and Zoe can be found in the just released KISSING GAMES and will return in the final book of the Kinloch series, MUSICAL GAMES out January 2023.

And Kelly has just released KEEP PARIS, a new standalone series starter, enemies to lovers with a second chance French twist.

But Tabi and Bax will return in RESIDUAL SUGAR - when Becca tries to get out of her own grumpy way and find her happily ever after, releasing early 2023.

All of our books can be found on Amazon and in Kindle Unlimited. Just click the titles above to link to our books and pre-orders.

If you'd like to spread the joy and wonder of the season then please write us a lovely review of Christmas Chaos on Amazon, Goodreads, Bookbub, and anywhere else you like! A review truly is the best gift you can give an author.

Thank you. Thank you. Thank you for reading and enjoying Christmas Chaos. Your reviewing means everything to us.

ALSO BY EVIE ALEXANDER & KELLY KAY

Evie & Kelly's Holiday Disasters

Volume One

Cupid Calamity

mybook.to/CupidCalamity

Cookout Carnage

mybook.to/CookoutCarnage

Christmas Chaos

mybook.to/ChristmasChaos

ABOUT EVIE ALEXANDER

Evie Alexander is an award-winning author of sexy romantic comedies with a very British sense of humour.

A self-confessed 'method writer', Evie has taken it upon herself to live a full and messy life, from which romantic and personal failures become fodder for her laugh-out-loud plotlines.

Imaginative, passionate and frequently called 'bonkers' by her friends, Evie's interests include reading, eating, saving the world, and fantasising about people who only exist between the pages of her books.

Her novel *Highland Games* won Best in Category in the The CHATELAINE Book Awards for Romantic Fiction and Women's Fiction 2021. Evie lives in the West country of the UK with her family, where she pens her steamy stories from the Smut Hut.

Also by Evie Alexander
Full-length Romantic Comedy Novels

THE KINLOCH SERIES
mybook.to/KinlochSeries

Highland Games
mybook.to/HighlandGames

Steamy, Small Town, Enemies-to-Lovers, Fish-out-of-Water, Grumpy/Sunshine, Opposites Attract, Scottish Highlands, Secret Identity

Hollywood Games
mybook.to/HollywoodGames
Steamy, Small Town, Soulmates, Grumpy/Sunshine, Hollywood, Scottish Highlands

Kissing Games
mybook.to/Kissinggames
Steamy, Small Town, Dark Secrets, Bodyguard/Actress, Forced Proximity, Dating Game, Fling, Afraid to Commit, Emotional Scars, Hollywood, Scottish Highlands

Musical Games
mybook.to/MusicalGames
Steamy, Small Town, Grumpy/Sunshine, Male Virgin, Cinnamon Roll Hero, Love/Hate, Opposites Attract, In Denial, Forced Proximity, Afraid to Commit, Emotional Scars, Hollywood, Scottish Highlands

Evie's website and newsletter sign up:
www.eviealexanderauthor.com

instagram.com/eviealexanderauthor
facebook.com/eviealexanderauthor
twitter.com/Evie_author
bookbub.com/authors/evie-alexander
amazon.com/Evie-Alexander/e/B08ZJGLP29?ref=sr_ntt_s-rch_lnk_1&qid=1630667484&sr=8-1
pinterest.com/eviealexanderauthor

ABOUT KELLY KAY

Kelly is the author of eleven funny and steamy contemporary romance full-length novels. Her most popular books revolve around her Five Families Vineyard Series which starts with Crushing.

She's a writer, married to a writer, mother of a creative dynamo of an twelve-year-old boy in Chicago, and currently looking for either a cup of coffee or a glass of wine. She's gotten very used to waking up to a Zoom call request from England. And Evie's gotten quite used to seeing Kelly's bedhead and her sucking down copious amounts of coffee as they dreamed up this bonkers project. Time Zones can be a bitch.

If you want to get to know the world of the Five Families' Vineyard Series better- you can find them here. A small-town found family interconnected standalone series set in Sonoma, CA

(Elle & Josh) https://mybook.to/Crushing
LaChappelle/Whittier Vineyard Trilogy: Crushing, Rootstock, Uncorked- enemies to lovers, forced proximity, workplace, billionaire, reformed bad boy, instalove/instahate

(Bax & Tabi) https://mybook.to/OverABarrel
Stafýlia Cellars Duet: Over A Barrel/Under the Bus – Friends to lovers, opposites attract, ticktock timeline, soulmates

(David & Nat) https://mybook.to/Meritage
Gelbert Family Winery Standalone: Meritage - Workplace, Reformed player, secret baby, single parent

(Becca & Brick) https://mybook.to/ResidualSugar – Coming 2023
Gelbert Family Winery Standalone: Residual Sugar - Reverse grumpy sunshine, forced proximity, Military Mercenary, marriage of convenience

(Sal & Poppy) – Coming 2023
Pietro Family Book One – Forbidden love, Mafia, secret life, opposites attract

(Sam & Sammy) – Coming soon
Langerford Cellars Book One – soulmates, destined love, second chance, rescue recovery

(Ingrid & Ian) - https://mybook.to/MeetCutes
Schroeder Estate Vineyards and Winery: Follow Me
A 5 Families/ChiTown Stories Crossover Novella found in *A Series of Unfortunate Meet Cutes Anthology* but to be rereleased with an extended epilogue- 2023 launching the Carriage House Chronicles

Other Kelly Kay books

ChiTown Stories

Shock Mount/Crossfade – A Lyrical Duet https://mybook.to/ShockMount

Present Tense https://mybook.to/PresentTense

For Keep Series

Keep Paris - Series Starter- NEW RELEASE https://mybook.to/KeepParis

Enemies to Lovers, workplace romance, close proximity with a second chance twist- Available Now!

Standalone

Side Piece – https://mybook.to/SidePiece

Insta love, workplace, secret past, romance

Kelly's website and newsletter sign up:
www.kellykayromance.com

MEDIA LINKS

Goodreads: https://tinyurl.com/KellyKgoodreads
Bingebooks: https://bingebooks.com/author/kelly-kay
Pinterest: https://www.pinterest.com/kellykaybooks/_saved/
Spotify: http://bit.ly/KellyKayPlaylists

instagram.com/kelly_kay_books
bookbub.com/profile/kelly-kay

ACKNOWLEDGMENTS

Evie and Kelly want to thank every one of you individually, but we're exhausted from finishing this epic series, so a general THANK YOU will have to do. Seriously, this has been such a fun and joyful experience creating this world together.

(This is Kelly writing right now)

Evie, thank you so much for following me down this rabbit hole. Writing these stories with you has been so mostly joyful and ultimately insanely rewarding. I adore you, my forever work wife, and I look forward to figuring out the next place to put our brand of chaos.

(This is Evie writing right now)

Kelly, thank you so much for not running a mile when I contacted you out of the blue all those years ago to sing your praises. Yes, I am bonkers, but you embraced the insanity and I am forever grateful. Working with you has been an absolute joy and I can't wait to continue the journey!

Together we want to thank those of you who jumped on our crazy train from the beginning:

Margaret Amatt, whose covers and support are dreamy and perfect and Marina for her fabulous illustrations.

Aimee Walker, our intrepid editor who was not only invested in the Holiday Disasters but in all of our characters who she shepherded to publication before Evie and Kelly even met. Rory, Zoe, Tabi, and Bax are your book babies. This one is for you because, besides us, you've known them the longest.

Mike Thomas, thank you for your keen eye and edits that kept the HD somewhat grounded. And for reminding us to indent and not indent and indent and not indent.

Victoria, Mandy, Taryn and Liezl at Emlin Press. Thank you for keeping the Holiday Disasters train moving so smoothly throughout the year and half we've been putting all of this together. Not sure how any of this could have been done without you.

The early readers, wow, do we love you and your advice, thoughts, and cheers from the sidelines: Allison, Julia, Margaret, Pash, Sandie and Tori.

Our families have put up with so much nonsense, and we're glad they knew we were crazy before we began all of this almost a year ago.

And again, we thank the readers who have embraced us in the past year. And to be honest, we're shocked there are so many of you who have loved Ben, Sabrina, Jonathan, Tristan, Rory, and Tabi as much as we do. You're all amazing and know that every word you've said whether it was word of mouth, a post like or a review has been the ultimate Holiday gift to us this year. Thank you. xo

Until next time,
    K&E

CPSIA information can be obtained
at www.ICGtesting.com
Printed in the USA
BVHW051132091122
651532BV00017B/403

9 781914 473135